Elizabeth Gail and the Mystery of the Hidden Key

Hilda Stahl

 Tyndale House Publishers, Inc.
Wheaton, Illinois

DEDICATED WITH GREAT LOVE TO
Bradley Allen of Freeport
Dawn Lee of P.E.I.
and
Eric Jason of Cleveland

Cover and interior illustration © 1992 by David Henderson
Text © 1992 by Word Spinners, Inc.

Library of Congress Cataloging-in-Publication Data

Stahl, Hilda.
    Elizabeth Gail and the hidden key mystery / Hilda Stahl.
        p.   cm — (Elizabeth Gail series ; no. 20)
    Summary: Twelve-year-old Libby learns how good it feels to follow
the Christian example of her foster family when she helps two boys
who are living in the shed behind her new father's store.
    ISBN 0-8423-0816-4
    [1. Christian life—Fiction.   2. Foster home care—Fiction.
3. Homeless persons—Fiction.] I. Title. II. Series: Stahl,
Hilda.   Elizabeth Gail series ; no. 20.
PZ7.S78244Ek i   1992
[Fic]—dc20   92-1031

Printed in the United States of America

97 96 95 94 93
7   6   5   4   3

Dear Reader:

Congratulations! You're about to go on a whole new adventure with Elizabeth Gail and her friends and family! Because this is an all new adventure, it is book #20. But the story actually takes place right after book #5, *Elizabeth Gail and Trouble at Sandhill Ranch.*

We hope you will enjoy reading about Elizabeth Gail and her great adventures. (A complete list of the exciting Elizabeth Gail books is shown below.) And keep your eyes open for more brand-new Elizabeth Gail books coming soon!

Contents

ONE
Libby's camera

Silently, Libby crouched in the barn with her camera aimed at the nest of kittens. A wisp of damp brown hair clung to Libby's flushed cheek. A fly buzzed around her ear, but she didn't swat it away. She dared not move even an inch! The newspaper was having a "Cute Animal Photo Contest," and Libby was sure she could win with a picture of the kittens. Libby's heart leaped. First prize was twenty-five dollars, and she planned to buy a new halter for Snowball, her horse. Never in Libby's twelve years had she won a prize or even entered a contest. Just then the mother cat walked away, leaving the kittens burrowed down in the hay. Just outside the barn, Snowball nickered and Goosy Poosy honked. Libby gripped the camera tightly and barely breathed as two yellow striped kittens peeked up over the hay. Their green eyes were big and round. One kitten mewed with its mouth open, its little sharp white teeth showing. The other one looked curious. Libby clicked the shutter, then jumped up with a laugh. "That should turn out great!"

"What should?" asked Ben as he stepped into the barn. His red hair was damp with sweat. His blue tee shirt and jeans were streaked with dirt. At thirteen, he was the oldest of the Johnson kids. And he was getting taller and thinner all the time.

Libby pointed to the kittens. "I've gotten about five shots of the kittens, but this last one was the best so far. I really think I have a chance to win, Ben!"

"Great!" Ben grinned as he scooped up a kitten and rubbed his cheek against its soft hair. "I heard some of the kids in my Sunday school class say they were entering, too."

"I know a lot of kids will send in pictures," Libby said. She sighed heavily, fingering the camera hanging down her thin chest. "Maybe I won't send mine in. They wouldn't want an ugly foster kid competing in the contest."

Ben frowned. "Cut it out, Elizabeth Gail Dobbs! You said you'd try not to think you're ugly and unwanted. We want you! As soon as your mother signs the papers, Mom and Dad will adopt you."

Libby nodded. "I know. Sometimes I get so scared when I think she might not sign. She doesn't want me, and she doesn't want anyone else to have me." Abruptly Libby pushed thoughts of Mother out of her mind. "Ben, I have the perfect halter picked out for Snowball. Dad got it in his store last week." It had taken Libby several weeks to call Chuck "Dad," but now it came easily.

Ben touched Libby's camera. "I'd like to use your camera this weekend when I go with Grandpa to the copper mine."

Libby's stomach turned over. She'd watched how careless Ben had been with his own camera. She didn't want anything to happen to hers. "I have to get ready to go to the store with Dad and Susan," Libby said, taking a step toward the barn door.

"Wait," said Ben, touching her arm. "Would you let me use your camera?"

Libby stiffened. She knew none of the Johnsons were selfish, and she knew Jesus wanted her to share. But she just couldn't let Ben take her precious camera! She'd saved her allowance, her baby-sitting money, and her paycheck from Chuck's store to buy the camera. She didn't want to take the chance that Ben would ruin it, like he'd ruined his own.

Ben looked at Elizabeth curiously. "What's wrong, Elizabeth?"

Libby shrugged. "I want to use the camera myself, Ben."

Ben set the kitten back in the nest. "I just need it a few days. Come on, Libby. Don't be so selfish!"

Libby lifted her pointed chin and her hazel eyes flashed. "I'm not selfish!" But she felt selfish. "You can't use my camera. I don't want you to."

Ben narrowed his eyes. "I'll tell Mom. She'll make you loan it to me," he said angrily. Then he pushed past Libby and ran into the bright morning sunlight.

Libby's heart sank as she ran after Ben. Suddenly, from out of nowhere, Goosy Poosy honked and ran toward Libby, his long white neck out and his white wings flapping. Libby screamed and ran faster. She ducked around Ben before the goose could knock her down again the way he had when Miss Miller had brought her to the Johnson farm last November.

Ben and Libby both stopped just inside the back porch. Libby tried to catch her breath, her chest rising and falling.

Ben glanced at Libby. He was still frowning angrily. "I'm telling, Mom," he said in a low voice, then stomped into the family room where they could hear Vera playing the piano.

"See if I care!" snapped Libby. But Libby did care. She hated to have any of the Johnsons mad at her.

Slowly Libby walked to the family room and

watched Vera play. Libby wanted to play the piano more than she'd ever wanted to do anything in her life. She took lessons, but she couldn't play nearly as well as Vera did.

When Vera finished the piece she was playing, she looked up at Ben. "What's wrong?" she asked when she saw his frowning face.

Ben shot a look at Libby. "Mom, Elizabeth won't let me borrow her camera for this weekend. Make her do it, will you?"

Vera slowly stood as she looked from Ben to Libby. Vera wore a pink, flowered blouse and faded jeans. She was slightly taller than Ben. "The camera does belong to Libby," said Vera.

"It does!" cried Libby. "I bought it myself."

"But I let her use my baseball glove in the last game, and I bought that with my own money," said Ben.

"He did, Libby," said Vera as she brushed back her blonde hair.

Libby moved restlessly. She smelled the yellow roses in the vase on the piano. She heard Kevin and Toby shouting to each other upstairs. The smell of breakfast coffee drifted in from the kitchen.

Vera rested her hands lightly on Libby's bony shoulders. "Libby, you know it's right to share."

"I know," Libby whispered.

"So share," said Ben sharply. "I need that camera for this weekend."

"I don't want him to ruin it," said Libby weakly.

"I won't ruin it!" cried Ben. "I promise, Elizabeth!"

"It's up to you, Libby," said Vera. "It is your camera, so I'll let you decide what to do."

Ben looked very smug as he sank to the piano bench and waited for Libby's answer.

Vera kissed Libby's cheek. "I love you, Libby. I'll love you no matter what decision you make."

Libby relaxed slightly. It was hard to imagine that Vera and Chuck loved her no matter what she did. They'd told her God had put a special love for her in their hearts when they'd first read her case history.

Just then the grandfather clock beside the front door bonged nine. "You'll have to hurry to get ready to go to the store, Libby," said Vera. "Chuck wants to leave soon."

Libby glanced at Ben, then looked away. "You can't use my camera, Ben," she finally said barely above a whisper. She kept her eyes glued to the fireplace across the room.

Ben leaped up. "That's not fair! I need a camera for this weekend!"

Vera turned to Ben and shook her finger at him. "You stop that! Libby made her decision, and you're not going to have a fit about it."

7

"I'll just go talk to Dad! He'll make her let me use it!" Ben ran into the hall and down to Chuck's study.

Libby's stomach fluttered. She looked helplessly at Vera, but she was walking toward the kitchen. "I won't let Ben use my camera no matter what Dad says," muttered Libby grimly. But she knew that wasn't true.

Suddenly Libby ran to the wide stairs and up to her room. She pushed the camera to the back of her closet shelf behind a board game.

In a flash Libby ran to the bathroom, quickly undressed, and stepped into the shower. She knew she wouldn't be able to hear Chuck calling her to his study. By the time she was out and dressed, it would be time to go to the store. He'd be too busy thinking about his day to say anything about the camera.

Back in her room, Libby pulled on blue shorts and a blue tee shirt with three yellow flowers appliquéd on the front of it. With trembling hands she brushed her hair and clipped it back with a long yellow banana clip.

Just then twelve-year-old Susan stuck her head in the door, her red-gold ponytails bobbing over each ear. She wore yellow shorts and a blue and yellow tee shirt. She, Ben, and Kevin were the real Johnson kids. Toby was adopted, and Libby was still just a foster kid.

8

Smiling, Susan said, "Dad says it's time to go, Libby."

"I'm ready," said Libby, forcing her voice to sound cheerful.

A couple of minutes later she ran with Susan to the pickup truck where Chuck was waiting. Ben stood beside the driver's door, and Libby's heart sank. She slowly slipped into the pickup after Susan.

"Right on time, girls," said Chuck with a wide smile. He had red hair with a touch of gray at the temples. He was dressed in a white shirt and gray dress pants. He turned back to Ben. "That's our final word on it, Ben. Don't bring it up again."

Ben sighed heavily, then slowly walked to the house with his head down and his shoulders bent.

Libby breathed easier.

"Don't bring what up?" asked Susan as Chuck started the pickup and drove down the long driveway.

Libby locked her hands in her lap.

"Ben wanted to borrow Elizabeth's camera," Chuck said. He glanced at Libby and smiled. "Mom and I said it was your decision, Elizabeth. And it is."

Libby tried to smile back, but she couldn't. She thought what Chuck said should make her feel better, but a heavy weight seemed to be pressing against her heart. Why did she feel so terrible?

TWO
The general store

Libby stood near the checkout counter and listened as Chuck gave them instructions for the day. She'd wanted to work in the section of the store where Chuck sold western wear and tack for horseback riding. Instead, he told them to stock shelves in the grocery section. Chuck's clerk, Mrs. Lois Crabtree, had been in the store since nine when it opened. She was busy waiting on a customer in the small section of toys and games. Libby could hear Mrs. Crabtree laugh. She had a strange cackle that made everyone giggle just to hear it. But it didn't make Libby giggle this time.

Chuck slipped his arms around Libby and Susan. "You girls work for two hours, then take a break. If I'm gone, help yourself to a snack from my office refrigerator."

Libby tried to smile at Chuck, but couldn't. Could he really continue to love her if she was selfish? Maybe she should've let Ben borrow her camera. If he ruined it, she'd make him buy her a new one. Her stomach turned. No! She wanted her very own camera that she'd bought with her own money!

Chuck kissed Libby's cheek, then Susan's. "Get to work, girls. Earn some money." He grinned and winked, then walked to his office, leaving the smell of his after-shave behind.

Libby followed Susan down the cereal and canned goods aisle to the storeroom in back. The smell of coffee beans was strong. The air-conditioning clicked on, blowing away the warm air. Mrs. Crabtree laughed again and Susan giggled. Libby bit her lip and forced back a sigh.

"Here's the box of soup we have to price," said Susan, nudging a cardboard box on the floor.

Libby found the pricing gun in the supply cupboard and fixed the correct price.

"How come you won't let Ben borrow your camera?" asked Susan as she opened the box of soup cans.

Libby's jaw tightened. "He's too careless."

Susan looked up at Libby in surprise. "Ben is? He's always careful!"

"He left his camera in the rain, and he even dropped it!"

"Toby left it in the rain," said Susan.

Libby swallowed hard as she bent over the box with the pricing gun.

"And Ben dropped it because it was slippery from something Toby put on it."

Libby's heart sank lower and lower. "I didn't know that."

"Now that you do, can Ben borrow the camera?"

Libby finished pricing the top layer of the box of soup. "I don't know," she finally said. She didn't want to tell Susan she'd never let Ben use the camera no matter what, or Susan would talk about it all day long.

"I wish I could go to the copper mine with Grandpa and Ben," said Susan with a big sigh. "I never get to do anything."

"You stayed a weekend with Grandma two weeks ago," said Libby as she lifted the box onto the cart. Libby had wanted to go, but it had been Susan's time alone with Grandma. Libby's turn would come later.

Susan talked about the copper mine as they stacked the soup onto the shelf. After they finished with the soup, they stacked cereal and juice.

Just then Mrs. Crabtree called, "Susan, could you come here a moment?"

Susan ran to Mrs. Crabtree at the front of the store while Libby emptied the last box. She wheeled the empty cardboard boxes to the storeroom and out the back door. The heat burned into her, and the bright sun almost blinded her. She walked past the storage shed, which was attached to the back of the store, and continued on to the edge of the parking lot. There, Libby pitched the empty boxes into the big blue dumpster. A movement to the side of the building caught her attention. She turned just in time to see two boys wearing red tee shirts slip around the corner to the front sidewalk.

Sweat stung Libby's eyes as she walked to the back door. She stepped inside and closed the door against the heat. She wiped her face with a paper towel and took a long drink from the water cooler. She didn't want to look for Susan or run into Chuck. Libby sighed. "Why did Ben even have to ask to use my camera?" she muttered. It had ruined her whole day.

Finally Libby walked to the corner of the store to look at the halter she wanted for Snowball. She carefully picked it up. It was made with strands of white rope braided together with red rope. Snowball would look even more beautiful than usual wearing that halter! Libby touched the rope and the silver rings and buckle. "I wish I could take it home today," she whispered.

Suddenly she felt someone watching her. She glanced around to see the two boys in red tee shirts looking at her. They were the same boys she'd seen outdoors. Their thin, dirty faces looked like they were about nine and ten years old. They ducked behind a rack of western shirts. Libby frowned. Why were the boys acting so strange? Maybe they were shoplifting. Just then the smaller boy poked his head around the shirt rack and stuck his tongue out at Libby. All the built-up anger toward Ben burst out toward the boy.

With a scowl Libby dropped the halter and ran down the aisle around the shirt rack. The boys weren't there. Her face flushed and her heart pounded as she ducked around another aisle. Where had the boys gone?

"Who cares anyway?" muttered Libby, giving up the chase. She stopped in front of the case that held camera film. Maybe she'd buy a roll of film today and take more pictures when she got home this after-noon. Maybe the ones of the kittens hadn't turned out as cute as she'd thought.

Libby started to walk away from the film case, and her toe hit something. She looked down to see an open pack of gum on the floor. With a frown she picked it up and slipped it in her pocket. She'd give it to Mrs. Crabtree.

Suddenly someone grabbed Libby's arm. She

gasped in fright and stared into the round face of an angry woman.

"I saw you shoplift that gum!" the woman cried. Her dark eyes blazed with anger. She was short and plump and wore a tight tee shirt and jeans. "It's brats like you that make the prices shoot through the ceiling! Come with me right now to see the owner."

Libby tried to speak as the woman jerked her hard to the front of the store. The woman didn't look at all like her real mother, but she sure sounded and acted like her. Libby's words caught in her throat, and shivers ran up and down her spine.

The woman shoved Libby at Mrs. Crabtree. "I caught this girl shoplifting!"

Mrs. Crabtree's blue eyes grew round. "You must be mistaken, Mrs. Crest. That's Libby."

"Just check her pocket if you don't believe me!" snapped Mrs. Crest. She reached into Libby's pocket and pulled out the gum, held it high, then slapped it on the checkout counter. "I told you!"

Libby shivered harder. She wanted to tell Mrs. Crabtree what had happened, but she couldn't force out the words.

"She's as guilty as sin!" cried Mrs. Crest. "Just look at her!"

Mrs. Crabtree cleared her throat as she pulled Libby to her side. "Mrs. Crest, Libby's dad is the owner of this store. She wouldn't shoplift. She works here." Mrs. Crabtree's voice was low and soothing. "I'd call her dad, but he stepped out for a few minutes and took his other daughter, Susan, with him."

Tears burned Libby's eyes at the gentle way Mrs. Crabtree spoke. Finally Libby found her voice. "The gum was on the floor already opened," she said hoarsely. "I picked it up to bring it to you."

Mrs. Crabtree patted Libby's arm. "Thank you, dear."

Mrs. Crest scowled. "How do you know she's telling the truth? This girl must be the foster kid the Johnson's took in. You can't trust foster kids."

Libby bit her trembling lip. Would she go her whole life having people treat her this way?

Mrs. Crabtree cleared her throat. "Mrs. Crest, I can take your things at the checkout counter if you're ready."

"I have a few items to pick up yet," said Mrs. Crest stiffly. She sniffed and walked away with her nose high in the air.

Libby brushed a hand across her eyes to wipe away her tears.

Mrs. Crabtree patted Libby's arm. "Don't let Mrs. Crest upset you further. She gets carried away sometimes."

Libby smiled shakily. "Thanks for helping me," she said softly.

Mrs. Crabtree nodded, but she couldn't say anything because another customer came up to the checkout.

Libby slowly walked toward Chuck's office. Just then she saw the two boys again. They didn't see her. As Libby watched, one boy stuck a candy bar under his tee shirt. Libby bit back a gasp. The other boy slipped a pack of peanut butter crackers into his pocket. Libby's heart almost jumped through her chest. Were the boys really shoplifting, or had they bought the things earlier? She would not embarrass them the way Mrs. Crest had embarrassed her! But if they were shoplifting, she couldn't let them get away with it.

Libby walked toward the back of the store, keeping her eye on the boys. Just then Mrs. Crest wheeled her cart around the aisle of paper products. Libby ducked out of sight behind a display case. She didn't want Mrs. Crest even to speak to her or the boys.

Mrs. Crest dropped a package of napkins into her cart and wheeled around another aisle out of sight just as the boys peeked around the canned goods aisle.

Libby held her breath and waited to see what the boys were going to do. One of them picked up a box

of crackers while the other grabbed a can of peaches. They looked around, then instead of walking to the front of the store, they slipped into the storeroom. Libby gasped and ran to the door after them. Just as she stepped into the storeroom, the outside door closed, and she knew the boys had gone outdoors. She raced across the room and jerked open the door, fully expecting to see the boys in the parking lot or running toward the house on the far side of the parking lot. But they had disappeared! She couldn't see them anywhere. She ran along the side of the store to the front sidewalk. She looked up and down but couldn't see any boys wearing red tee shirts.

Slowly Libby walked back inside. She knew she'd have to tell Mrs. Crabtree about the boys. But when Libby saw Mrs. Crest at the checkout, she slipped out of sight again. Finally Mrs. Crest walked out. Before Libby could move, the two boys came to the checkout counter with a loaf of bread and a package of bologna. Libby blinked in surprise.

"Hi, Bobby. Hi, Mike," said Mrs. Crabtree with a wide smile.

"We only have three dollars," said Bobby as he flipped his dirty hair out of his eyes.

Mrs. Crabtree smiled at them. "I guess I can put in the rest," she said. "You're both such good little customers and so helpful all the time."

Libby bit back a cry. Good little customers? They were shoplifters!

"Thank you, Mrs. Crabtree," said Mike, smiling.

Libby took a step forward, then stopped. Should she tell Mrs. Crabtree now in front of the boys, or should she wait to tell her after they left?

THREE
The halter

Trembling, Libby watched Bobby and Mike walk out
of the store. The minute the door closed after them
Libby cried, "Mrs. Crabtree, those boys!"

Mrs. Crabtree smiled. "Aren't they precious?
They've been coming in now for a couple of months.
They help me a lot. Sweep the sidewalks. Carry out
bags when customers need help. Just a lot of little
things. I've grown to love them like my own grand-
sons."

The words died in Libby's throat. She couldn't tell
Mrs. Crabtree the truth about the boys and break her
heart. "Excuse me, please, but I have to go outside a
minute." Libby dashed out and frantically looked
around for the boys. They had disappeared into thin
air. "Where are they?" Libby lifted her hands in
defeat and dropped them at her sides. The hot sum-

mer sun burned into her, but she didn't notice. Rock music blared from a black pickup driving past.

With a tired sigh Libby turned to walk back inside. Before she'd taken two steps she heard her name called. She turned and her heart sank. It was Brenda Wilkens! Libby had been trying for months to be kind to her, but Brenda made it very hard.

Her long dark hair flipped around her slender shoulders as Brenda Wilkens ran toward Libby. "What are you doing in town, Libby Dobbs?"

"Working here," said Libby, motioning toward the store.

"Does Chuck Johnson actually trust you to work there?" asked Brenda in surprise.

Libby knotted her fist, but she knew Jesus didn't want her to punch Brenda in the nose the way she had one other time. "What are you doing in town?" Libby asked as politely as she could.

"Mom and I are shopping," said Brenda. "Joe's at the Johnson farm riding horses with Ben. I was going to stay, too, but Mom promised to buy me new jeans."

Libby glanced around for Mrs. Wilkens. "Where is your mom?"

"She stopped in the drug store, but she'll be here in a minute. I'm going to look at the jeans while I'm waiting for her." Brenda pushed open the heavy door and walked ahead of Libby into the store. "Since you're working here, you can wait on me," Brenda said with a smug look on her face.

A muscle tightened in Libby's cheek. She glanced around for Mrs. Crabtree but saw she was busy with two customers. As kindly as she could, Libby asked, "What size jeans do you wear?"

Brenda told her as she stopped at the western wear. "Dad said he might get horses for me and Joe to show this summer. So I need riding pants and a shirt too. Maybe even a hat." Brenda picked up a broad-brimmed, light blue hat and tried it on.

Libby burst out laughing before she could stop herself.

Brenda glared at her. "What's so funny?"

"I guess you don't seem the type to wear a cowboy hat."

Brenda lifted her chin. "I can wear one if I want!" She dropped the blue hat back in place and tried on a black one.

"That's better," said Libby, but Brenda still looked like a city girl trying to look country. The Wilkens family lived near the Johnson farm, but they were really city people.

Just then Susan walked up. "Hi," she said to Libby and Brenda.

Libby smiled wide. She was never so glad to see

anyone. "Hi, Susan! You're just in time to wait on Brenda." Libby wanted to walk away, but she didn't want Susan to have to be with Brenda alone.

"Dad said he'd buy us horses," said Brenda with a flip of her long hair. "Joe and I'll show them and win all kinds of awards."

Libby bit back a groan. She wanted to say Brenda couldn't show a horse if she tried, but she knew Jesus wanted her to be kind. Sometimes it was very hard to be a Christian!

Brenda walked to the tack and looked at bits and bridles and halters. She picked up the very halter Libby planned to buy.

Libby caught her breath but didn't say a word. If Brenda knew Libby wanted to buy the halter, Brenda would buy it just to be mean.

Susan reached over and touched the halter Brenda held. "It's pretty, isn't it? Libby is going to buy it for Snowball."

Libby's stomach knotted and she stared at Susan, silently trying to tell her to keep quiet. But Susan didn't notice.

Brenda held the halter higher and studied it as if it was a great work of art. "This is a nice halter. I'll buy it." She looked right at Libby.

"You can't have it!" Libby grabbed the halter from

Brenda and held it tight to her. "It's mine!" Libby's voice rose. "And you know it, Brenda Wilkens!"

Susan caught Libby's arm. "Shhh! Do you want the whole store to hear you?"

Brenda's dark eyes flashed. "Give that back to me right now! It's for sale, and I am a customer!"

Mrs. Crabtree hurried to the girls with her face flushed. "Girls, girls! What's going on? Susan? Libby? You know your dad doesn't let you get loud in here."

Libby was too angry to lower her voice. She held the halter up. "Brenda thinks she can buy this! But I'm going to."

Mrs. Crabtree's face turned even redder as she glanced around at the other customers. "Libby, please honey, keep your voice down. Now, what's this all about?"

Susan twisted her fingers together. "Both the girls want the same halter."

"It's mine!" snapped Libby.

Brenda shook her head. "I am the customer. The halter was right there for sale, so I am going to buy it."

Mrs. Crabtree sighed heavily, then reached for the halter. "Give it here, Libby. We can order another one for you."

"But I want this one!" cried Libby. She was afraid they'd never be able to get one just like it.

"Stop it, Libby!" snapped Susan. "Don't be such a spoiled, selfish brat!"

Tears sprang to Libby's eyes, and she quickly turned away. She was not being spoiled or selfish because she wanted the very halter she'd picked out to buy! Why couldn't Susan see that?

Brenda nudged Libby and whispered, "I hope you never get a halter like this."

Libby pressed her fists to her sides and bit her tongue to keep back a flood of angry words as Brenda followed Mrs. Crabtree to the checkout counter.

Susan gripped Libby's arm. "What's wrong with you today? First you won't let Ben use your camera, and now you fight over a halter with a customer."

"Not just any customer!" hissed Libby. "That was Brenda Wilkens! And if you'd kept your big mouth shut, she wouldn't have wanted Snowball's halter!"

Susan's eyes widened and slowly filled with tears. "Why are you blaming me? What did I do?"

All the anger drained from Libby and she said, "It doesn't matter now." She glanced around. "Where's Dad?"

"He had a meeting with the mayor, but he'll be back before one." Susan brushed a tear off her cheek. "I'm sorry Brenda bought the halter, Libby. And I'm sorry for calling you a spoiled, selfish brat. I know you're not."

"I'm sorry I got so mad at you." Libby smiled weakly. It always surprised her that the Johnsons could apologize so easily. Libby had to force out an apology if she was told to make one. Just then she thought of Bobby and Mike. "I wish Dad would hurry back," Libby said.

"Why?" asked Susan.

"Let's go to the storeroom and I'll tell you."

"Dad said he wanted us to straighten up the storeroom," said Susan as they walked to the door.

In the storeroom Libby told Susan about the boys. "They took stuff right off the shelves and then walked through that door and outside."

Susan frowned. "That's terrible! Did you tell Mrs. Crabtree?"

"I was going to, but she loves those boys and they're nice to her. I just couldn't do it."

Susan walked to the back door and opened it. "It's unlocked most of the time, so the boys could get in and out any time they want. We have to tell Dad."

"I know." Libby looked past Susan into the parking lot. Heat waves rose from the parking lot pavement. Libby ducked around Susan and stepped outdoors. The hot sidewalk burned through the soles of her sneakers. She walked toward the storage shed, then stopped and looked around. A robin dusted itself in the dirt under a tall oak tree.

"Maybe the boys live around here," said Susan as she looked toward the houses along the street in back of the parking lot.

A great sadness welled up on the inside of Libby. "Susan, why would those boys shoplift? Do you think they could live on the street? Maybe they're starving."

Susan gasped. "Oh, that would be terrible! I've seen the homeless people on TV—even kids!"

Libby glanced up the street at the row of stores. At the other end of town was the big shopping mall. "Are there street people in this town?"

"Dad says so, but I've never seen them," said Susan, looking around.

"I wish we could find homes for all of them!" cried Libby.

"Me too," whispered Susan as tears welled up in her blue eyes.

Finally Libby walked back into the cool storeroom. "I guess we better get back to work. There's nothing we can do for the street people."

Susan picked up an empty box. "I'm going to ask Dad. He might know of something."

Libby nodded. She knew Chuck did a lot to help others. But maybe he'd be so upset by the two boys who had shoplifted that he wouldn't want to talk about the homeless. Then Libby smiled. Chuck was never too upset or too busy to help others. He was like Jesus. "And that's how I want to be," whispered Libby as she picked up the broom to sweep the floor.

FOUR
The hidden key

Libby stood in the shade just outside the back door. She was tired and thirsty after cleaning the store-room. She turned to Susan beside her. "Did Brenda really buy my halter?"

Susan nodded with a sad look on her face. "I heard her telling her mom she had to have it even if they didn't have a horse yet."

Libby sighed heavily. "I wanted that halter so much!"

"Dad will order another one. It takes only a few days to get the order."

"OK." With her hands behind her, Libby leaned against the store. The red bricks felt rough. Just then she touched a loose brick. "Look, Susan." Libby tugged gently, and the brick slid right out. Behind it she found a dull silver key. Trembling, she lifted it out.

"That's strange," whispered Susan. "I wonder what it's to."

Libby tried the back door, but it didn't fit. She glanced toward the storage shed. A tiny shiver trickled down her spine. With Susan close beside her she walked to the shed and tried the key in the lock. It slipped easily in place. Libby shot a look at Susan.

"Open it," whispered Susan.

Libby's mouth felt bone dry. Slowly she turned the key. It turned all the way, unlocking the door. "Why would Dad hide the key in such a strange place?" asked Libby.

"Maybe he didn't hide it there," said Susan, shivering.

Libby slowly pushed open the door. Heat rushed out along with a smell of chocolate. A half-eaten, melting candy bar lay on top of a cardboard box. Two sleeping bags were rolled up and stacked in a corner beside a box of food and a box of clothes.

Susan gasped. "Somebody lives in here!"

Libby tugged at the neck of her tee shirt, which suddenly seemed too tight. "Does Dad know?"

"I bet he doesn't. He'd never let anyone live in the storage shed!" Susan backed away from the open door. "It feels like we're peeking into someone's window."

"It does, doesn't it?" Libby slowly closed the door

and locked it. She looked at the key in her hand. Should she hide it again or give it to Chuck? Finally she tucked it back where she'd found it and slipped the brick in place. "Nobody would even know it's there," she whispered.

"It's so scary," said Susan, her face pale. "Who would live in a storage shed?"

"The homeless," said Libby hoarsely.

Susan nodded, her hand trembling at her throat. "If we tell Dad, he'll make them leave."

"I know."

Libby moved restlessly. "What'll we do?"

"We could find out who's living there and try to help," said Susan.

"Will we keep this a secret?"

"I won't tell anyone," whispered Susan, her eyes flashing with excitement.

"Me neither." Slowly Libby walked inside the store, Susan close on her heels. Libby saw Chuck at the stack of boxes and she jumped.

Chuck turned, then smiled. "I wondered where you girls were." He looked at their faces for a moment. "Is something wrong?"

"No," said Susan quickly.

Libby remembered the boys and quickly told Chuck about them. "Mrs. Crabtree might know where they live, but I didn't ask her."

Chuck nodded. "I've seen those boys. I never would've suspected them of shoplifting. They're nice boys. Mrs. Crabtree will take this hard. It was kind of you not to say anything to her, Libby. I'll handle it myself." Chuck stabbed his fingers through his red hair. "I sure hate to break her heart. But we can't have the boys shoplifting."

"Maybe they live on the street," said Susan.

"I doubt it," said Chuck. "They don't seem to be homeless."

"If I see them again, I'll find out where they live," said Libby.

Chuck nodded. "I guess I'd better go talk to Mrs. Crabtree now." He smiled at the girls. "Cheer up, you two. It's kind of you to be so concerned about Mrs. Crabtree's feelings, but there's nothing to be so sad about."

Libby felt a flush creep up her neck. She was thinking about the people who lived in the shed, not the two boys, but she couldn't tell Chuck that.

Susan moved closer to Libby, but she didn't say anything.

"Dad, what do you keep in the storage shed out back?" asked Libby, forcing her voice to sound normal.

"Nothing important. I haven't opened it in

months. Why?" asked Chuck, cocking a red brow questioningly.

Libby shrugged.

"Do you have the key?" asked Susan.

"Somewhere," said Chuck. "Maybe it's in my desk drawer in my office."

"Could we get it and look inside the shed?" asked Libby, forcing back a shiver.

"Sure. It's probably dusty and dirty in there, so don't get messy." With a smile Chuck walked from the room.

When the door closed behind him, Susan whispered, "I thought he'd read my mind!"

Libby nodded. At times it seemed Chuck could look right inside her head and know what she was going to do or say next.

"Let's go look inside the shed again," whispered Susan. "Maybe we can find something that will show us who's living there."

Libby's pulse leaped and she nodded as she walked oudoors with Susan.

Susan pulled the brick free and reached for the key. It was gone! Susan gasped and turned to Libby. "It's gone," she whispered weakly.

Libby looked toward the shed and stepped closer to Susan. "Maybe someone's inside the shed right

34

now. What if he's waiting to jump out at us and hurt us?"

"That only happens on TV," said Susan, shivering.

Libby didn't argue, but she knew it happened in real life. A man had been hurt in an apartment near where she and her real mother had lived. Libby had had nightmares for weeks afterward. "Maybe we shouldn't open the door," she said hoarsely.

"I'm not afraid!" Susan ran to the shed and tried to turn the knob, but it wouldn't budge. "It's still locked."

Libby shivered. "Someone took the key out of hiding. Maybe they saw us find it! Maybe they don't live in the shed, but want to break in!"

Trembling, Susan gripped Libby's arm. "Let's get Dad's key and open the door," she whispered.

Libby nodded, her mouth dry and her heart racing.

A few minutes later Libby peered into Chuck's middle drawer while Susan looked in a side drawer. "I don't see a key like the one to the shed."

"The one we found was probably a duplicate, so look for a brass key," said Susan.

Libby pushed aside paper clips, thumb tacks, several keys, and a few rubber bands.

Just then Mrs. Crabtree walked in, then stopped short. "Does your dad know you're in his desk?" she asked sharply.

Libby nodded.

Susan said, "We're looking for the key to the storage shed. Do you know where it is?"

Mrs. Crabtree thought for a moment. "Sometimes Chuck hangs keys on a key ring behind the door." She closed the door and peered at the wooden key rack. "This could be to the shed."

With butterflies fluttering in her stomach, Libby took the key. "Do you know what's in the shed?" she asked.

Mrs. Crabtree shook her head. "I've never looked inside." She glanced from Libby to Susan. "Are you girls going exploring?"

"Yes," they said together.

Mrs. Crabtree cleared her throat. "Girls, your dad told me about Bobby and Mike." She looked ready to cry. "It makes me feel so terrible for them and for us!"

"I'm sorry," said Susan.

"We'll see if we can talk to the boys and get them to stop shoplifting," said Libby.

"Your dad doesn't want them in the store again," said Mrs. Crabtree sadly. "I'll miss them so much!"

Libby wished she could do something to make Mrs. Crabtree feel better, but she didn't know what to do. "Do you know where they live?"

Mrs. Crabtree nodded. "Bobby told me. 1590 Lilac Circle."

Libby shot Susan a look and Susan nodded slightly. "We'll go talk to them. We have our work all done."

"I know where Lilac Circle is," said Susan. "It's a really nice part of town."

"Those boys wouldn't shoplift just to do it," said Mrs. Crabtree. She shook her head sadly. "There's more to this than meets the eye."

"We'll go in just a few minutes," said Libby. First she wanted to look in the shed again.

"Is Dad still here?" asked Susan.

"No. He had to leave again, but he'll be back in an hour or so," said Mrs. Crabtree.

"Tell him we're at Lilac Circle if he gets back before we do," said Libby. Mrs. Crabtree nodded.

Libby ran with Susan outdoors to the storage shed. Libby tried the key, but it wouldn't turn. Disappointed, she slipped the key into her pocket. "I thought sure it was the right one," she said. "It looks like it."

Susan ran to the brick. "I'm going to check again." She pulled the brick out, then gasped and stared inside at the key.

Libby peered over Susan's shoulder. "I can't believe it," Libby whispered hoarsely.

Her hand shaking, Susan lifted out the key. Slowly she walked to the shed and unlocked the door. Her face pale, she looked at Libby, then pushed open the door.

Libby felt the heat rush out as she looked inside. The candy bar was gone, but otherwise the shed looked the same.

"Should we go inside?" whispered Susan.

Libby hesitated and finally nodded. She stepped inside and the heat pressed against her. Sweat poured over her body. How could anyone live in here? It was too hot and the air too stale!

Susan looked at the box of clothes but didn't touch them.

Just under the edge of a sleeping bag Libby saw a brown teddy bear about ten inches long with most of its stuffing gone. She picked it up. The fur was rubbed off its stomach where it had been stitched shut, and one eye was missing. She held it up for Susan to see. The bear drooped in her hand. A lump lodged in Libby's throat. "A little kid lives in here," whispered Libby hoarsely. "What will we do, Susan?"

Susan touched the bear's tiny black nose. "We must learn who's staying here so we can help them."

Libby nodded. She put the bear back where she'd found it and slowly walked outdoors.

FIVE
1590 Lilac Circle

Libby walked beside Susan along Lilac Circle. Giant maple trees lined the street, shielding them from the hot sun. Houses with broad green lawns dotted with bright flowers stood back from the street.

"There it is!" cried Susan, pointing to a large, two-story white house with a copper-colored roof. Large copper-colored numbers were on the side of the house next to the wide front door.

"I hope we can talk to Bobby and Mike right now and take care of everything," said Libby as they walked up the sidewalk and around to the back door.

"Why would boys living in a house like this steal?" asked Susan.

Libby shook her head. She pushed the doorbell just as a honeybee landed on a big daisy nearby. A small, tan dog from next door yapped at the fence between the yards.

A woman about Vera's age jerked open the door, her brown eyes wide in her pale, oval face. She wore blue slacks and a white cotton blouse. When she saw Libby and Susan, her shoulders slumped and she looked disappointed. "Yes?" she said weakly.

"We're looking for Bobby and Mike," said Libby.

"Are they home?" asked Susan.

"Why do you want them?" asked the woman, suddenly alert again.

"Are you their mother?" asked Libby.

The woman nodded, and her brown hair bounced on her slender shoulders. "I'm Lorna Huntington. What about my boys?"

"I'm Libby, and this is Susan." Libby tried to look around Lorna Huntington to see into the house, but all she could see was a hallway. "Could we talk to Bobby and Mike?"

Lorna Huntington shrugged, looking defeated and tired again. "They're not here right now. But I'm expecting them back any time now."

"Could we wait?" asked Susan.

"No!" Lorna said nervously as she fingered the necklace at her throat. "I'm afraid that wouldn't be a good idea. Run along now. And if you see Bobby and Mike, tell them to hurry home."

"We saw them this morning," said Libby.

Lorna gasped and leaned against the doorframe. "This morning? Where?"

"At Chuck's General Store downtown," said Susan.

Tears welled up in Lorna's eyes. "Downtown? This morning? I had no idea they'd be downtown!"

"Is something wrong?" asked Susan softly. "Could we help?"

Lorna shook her head and looked as if she was struggling hard to pull herself together. "If you see them, tell them to please hurry home."

"We will," said Libby. Before she could say anything more, Lorna Huntington closed the door. Libby turned to Susan. "I wonder what's going on? She acted strange, didn't she?"

Susan nodded. "We have to talk to Bobby and Mike! I think we should walk down the street and wait in that park we saw."

"We can't be away from the store too long or Dad will worry." Libby sighed heavily as they walked toward the park. The neighborhood was very quiet. "I wish the boys would come right now so we could talk to them."

Just then a dark blue BMW drove past, and Libby glanced toward it. "There goes Mrs. Huntington!" Libby gasped. "She can't be expecting the boys like she said."

"That's very strange." Susan narrowed her eyes. "Why would she leave home now?"

"And why would she lie to us?" Libby sighed heavily. "We might as well go back to the store." She looked both ways and crossed the quiet street. "What if we can't find the boys today? We won't even be in town tomorrow to try again."

"We could ask Ben and Kevin to trade days with us," said Susan.

"That's a great idea!" Libby laughed and nodded as she walked around a red tricycle in the middle of the sidewalk. But then she remembered how mean she had been to Ben that morning and the laugh died in her throat. Ben might not want to trade days with her since she wouldn't let him borrow her camera. She bit her lower lip. It was very important for her to come to the store tomorrow. She'd have to ask Ben anyway. She shivered even in the heat.

Later, Libby wiped sweat off her forehead as they reached the parking lot beside the store. Suddenly she stopped. "Susan, look!" she cried, pointing to a dark blue BMW. "It's Mrs. Huntington's car!"

"It sure is! I think we have a mystery to solve." Susan laughed. "This is great! Finally I get to help solve a mystery!"

Just then Libby saw a flash of red disappear

behind the store. She gripped Susan's arm to silence her. "I think I just saw the boys," Libby whispered.

Susan's eyes sparkled, and her cheeks turned bright pink. "Where? Let's talk to them right now!"

Libby ran along the side of the store with Susan beside her. Libby reached the end of the building first and looked around it. There was no sign of the boys. "How can they disappear so fast?"

"Maybe you didn't see them," said Susan, sounding very disappointed.

"Maybe," said Libby, but she was almost positive she had. "Let's go inside and see what Mrs. Huntington is doing here." Libby suddenly shivered. What *was* Mrs. Huntington doing here?

Libby walked through the back door with Susan right behind her. They saw Mrs. Huntington talking with Mrs. Crabtree at the checkout counter. Libby turned to Susan and put a finger to her lips.

Susan nodded, her eyes dancing with excitement.

Libby led the way down the aisle and stopped behind a display with Susan right beside her. Libby wanted to listen to the women without them seeing her. She knew it wasn't right to eavesdrop, but she had to know what Mrs. Huntington was saying. Libby was glad no one else was in the store. She wondered where Chuck was but pushed aside thoughts of him while she listened to the two women.

"I know it's hard to hear what your boys did," Mrs. Crabtree said. "I would feel bad if I knew my children were shoplifting."

Mrs. Huntington looked ready to cry. "I can't imagine why they'd do such a terrible thing. Are you sure they're my Bobby and Mike?"

"I told you they're the very boys in the picture you showed me," said Mrs. Crabtree, looking very sad.

"Yes, of course. You did tell me." Mrs. Huntington sighed and dabbed at her eyes with a white tissue. "If you see the boys, will you please call me immediately, and I'll come get them."

Mrs. Crabtree nodded.

Mrs. Huntington pulled a checkbook from her purse. "I'll give you a hundred dollars," she said as she wrote out the check. "It should pay for what the boys took."

Libby bit back a gasp. She felt Susan stiffen beside her.

"Thank you. I'll tell Chuck Johnson. He'll be glad you paid. But we don't know if it came to that much." Mrs. Crabtree rang up the money on the cash register and handed the receipt to Mrs. Huntington. "I feel bad about the boys," Mrs. Crabtree continued as she pushed back a strand of hair with an unsteady hand. "They're very dear to me. I can't imagine them doing such a thing."

"We've been having family problems," said Mrs. Huntington. "Maybe they're stealing for attention, you know."

Mrs. Crabtree nodded. "It's sad. I wish I could get them to talk to me."

Mrs. Huntington nodded. "They always talked to their father, but they couldn't seem to open up to me."

"That's a shame. I liked the times with my kids." Mrs. Crabtree blinked tears from her eyes. "It's lonely now that they're grown and have homes of their own."

Libby eased back and motioned for Susan to follow. They slipped into the back room, then outdoors. The shade from the store building kept the hot sun off them.

"Something's not right with Mrs. Huntington's story," said Libby.

"What isn't?" asked Susan.

Libby shook her head. If Mrs. Huntington were Mother, Libby would know what was wrong. Libby's heart turned over. What if Mrs. Huntington beat and starved the boys? Maybe that's why they stole food.

Just then the storage shed door opened a crack. Libby almost jumped out of her sneakers.

Susan gripped Libby's arm, and her fingers dug into Libby's flesh.

Libby felt as if she were in a dream.

SIX
The surprise in the shed

Libby's spine tingled as the shed door opened even wider. A boy in a red tee shirt looked out. Libby sucked in her breath. It was Bobby Huntington!

"Bobby," whispered Susan without moving.

Bobby saw them and jumped back inside. The shed door slammed shut.

Libby leaped toward the shed with Susan close behind. Libby grabbed the knob, but the door was locked. Her mouth felt bone dry. She rapped on the door. "Open up, Bobby Huntington!"

"Open the door right now!" cried Susan, pounding the door with her fist.

"Get away from here," said Bobby, his voice muffled through the door.

"Your mother's here," said Libby in a hushed voice.

"No! Oh no!" cried Bobby. "Mike, Mom's here!"

"She can't take me!" shouted Mike.

Libby and Susan stared at each other in astonishment. In the distance a police siren wailed. Nearby a car backfired. Finally Libby leaned her face against the door and said quietly, "Bobby, open the door and let us in. We want to help you."

"Get away from here!" Bobby said, sounding close to tears.

"We won't tell anyone about you," said Libby. She suddenly felt frightened for the boys. "Just let us in to talk to you."

"No!" cried Bobby.

"Listen to me, Bobby," said Susan softly with her red-gold head against the door. "Libby and I want to help you. We won't do anything to hurt you."

"We won't tell your mom we found you," said Libby. Her hazel eyes sparkled with unshed tears. "You can trust us. You can! Please, Bobby, open the door. Hurry before your mom comes out of the store to her car."

Bobby opened the door and said weakly, "Come in. But there's not much room."

Libby stepped in and staggered at the heat and stale smell. She moved aside for Susan to come in.

His brown eyes wide with alarm, Mike huddled against a rolled sleeping bag with the small teddy bear clasped to his heart. His blond hair clung damply to his round head. "I won't go with her. You can't make me. I won't go with her." He sounded tired as if he'd said the same words many times before.

"How did you find out who we are?" asked Bobby with a scowl.

Libby glanced at Susan, then back to the boys. "I saw you shoplifting."

Bobby flushed, and Mike dropped his head.

Libby and Susan sat down on a rolled sleeping bag as they quickly told the boys the story. "So, tell me why you're in here instead of home with your mom," said Libby as she studied the frightened boys.

"We want to stay with Dad," said Mike. He looked close to tears as he clung to his teddy bear.

"Where is he?" asked Susan, looking around as if she could see him hiding under the sleeping bag or behind a stack of boxes.

"He's at work," said Bobby, twisting the tail of his red tee shirt around his dirty fingers.

"Does he work here in town?" asked Libby.

"I don't know," said Bobby while Mike shrugged his skinny shoulders.

"Are your parents divorced?" asked Susan.

The boys nodded sadly.

"Who has custody of you?" asked Libby. Her parents had not been divorced. Her real dad had just walked out on them when she was three years old. She pushed the terrible memory aside and waited for the boys to answer.

"Mom has," said Mike sadly.

"But we miss Dad too much," said Bobby. "So we looked for him until we found him. Now we live with him."

"Where does he live?" asked Susan.

"Here," said Bobby.

"Here in town?" asked Libby with a slight frown.

Bobby nodded. "Here," he said, pointing to where he was sitting.

Libby gasped.

Susan cried, "Not here!"

"But why does your dad live *here?*" asked Libby as she brushed sweat off her forehead.

Bobby rubbed his nose with the back of his hand, leaving a smudge of dirt at the round tip of his nose. "Dad lost his job after the divorce. He didn't have enough money for a place to live and for child support. He lives here for free."

"But he can't live here!" cried Susan, spreading her arms wide. "There's no bathroom or kitchen. And it's too hot in here!"

Libby thought of all the terrible places she'd lived, but none of them had been this small. She'd always had a bathroom and a kitchen! Susan had never lived anywhere but in the house she lived in now. It was a big, beautiful house with six bedrooms and four bathrooms and more windows than she could count. The kitchen was as big as four storage sheds put together!

Bobby wiped the sweat off his face with the tail of his red tee shirt. "Dad said once he gets a job that pays better, we'll live in an apartment."

"But I don't want a room of my own," said Mike stubbornly, his damp face pale. "I get scared in the dark."

"You and I will share a room," said Bobby gently.

"Your mom is really worried about you," said Susan.

Bobby's lip quivered. "We didn't want to leave, but she got mad at Dad and wouldn't let us see him."

"Maybe if you tell her how you feel, she'd change her mind," said Libby. It was hard for her to say that because she knew she could never trust Mother. Maybe the boys shouldn't trust their mother either. But if she was like Vera Johnson, they could trust her. Was Mrs. Huntington like Vera Johnson or like Mother? It was something she and Susan would have to find out.

"Mom won't listen to us," said Bobby. "She's too mad at Dad."

"Real mad," said Mike, nodding hard.

Suddenly Susan jumped up. Just having her move

made the space seem even smaller. "We are going to help you boys! I don't know what we'll do, but we'll help you."

Bobby reached for Susan's arm. "Don't tell Mom where we are," he said in alarm.

"We won't," Libby said. She noticed Susan didn't say anything. Did Susan have a plan?

"When does your dad get here?" asked Susan.

"After five," said Bobby.

"Maybe our dad could talk to him," said Susan.

Libby nodded. "That's a great idea!"

Bobby shook his head. "No! You can't do that! We'd get in big trouble!" Bobby looked helplessly from Libby to Susan. "Dad said we couldn't tell anyone we lived here. He said if we did, we'd have to go back to Mom."

"I won't go back to Mom," said Mike, shaking his head as he jumped up. "I mean it, Bobby!"

"I know, Mike." Bobby turned to Susan. "Don't tell your dad! Please, don't!"

Susan sighed, but finally agreed. "I hate to have you stay here!"

"We don't mind much," said Bobby. "Dad leaves the door open at night, and it cools off in here. And we go to the park a lot."

Just then Libby heard Chuck calling them. Libby sucked in her breath, and the boys shivered.

"It's Dad," said Susan weakly.

"Don't answer him," said Bobby in a voice so low Libby could barely hear.

"We won't," said Libby. How she hated not answering Chuck! She heard him call again.

"We have to go," Libby whispered. She pressed her ear to the door and waited until she heard Chuck close the back door of the store. Slowly she opened the shed door and peered outside, blinking against the bright sunlight. No one was in sight. She whispered good-bye to the boys and slipped out like a shadow with Susan close behind. The air was still hot, but it felt better than the closed-in air in the shed.

A minute later Libby found Chuck standing outside his office. There were no customers and Mrs. Crabtree sat behind the checkout counter with a can of orange pop in her hand. Libby said, "We heard you call, Dad."

"I've decided to go home now," Chuck said. "Business is really slow."

"Oh no!" cried Susan.

Libby's heart sank. They'd wanted to talk with Mr. Huntington to see if they could find a way to help. Now they'd have to wait.

"Are you sure you want to leave now?" asked

Susan. "Maybe a whole lot of customers will come flooding in."

Chuck laughed and tugged one of Susan's red-gold ponytails. "I thought you'd be glad to get back to the farm where it's cooler."

"We want to come again tomorrow," said Susan.

"We do," said Libby. Maybe tomorrow she could talk to Mr. Huntington.

"You'll have to talk to Ben and Kevin about tomorrow," said Chuck as he rattled his keys and change in his pockets. "If they want to change with you, it's fine with me."

Libby sighed. Would Ben agree to change time with them if he was still mad at her?

SEVEN
Susan's plan

Libby's heart jumped as Chuck stopped at the Fast Photo. She'd forgotten about the film they'd dropped off this morning. Suddenly she couldn't wait to see the pictures she'd taken for the "Cute Animal Photo Contest."

"You girls wait here," said Chuck as he slipped from the pickup truck. "I'll be right back."

Libby smiled and locked her hands together in her lap as Chuck walked away.

Susan turned to Libby with a bubbly laugh. "I just thought of a great plan!"

"For the contest?" asked Libby.

"No," said Susan, shaking her head, "I thought of a plan to help Bobby and Mike."

"Oh! That's great! What is it?"

"We'll buy them groceries with our own money." Susan looked very proud of herself.

Libby's heart sank. She had plans for every penny of hers.

"I have fifteen dollars saved," said Susan. "How about you, Libby?"

"I have twelve." Libby couldn't tell Susan she didn't want to spend it. Susan would really call her selfish. And it would be true!

"That would buy a lot of groceries!" Susan's eyes sparkled with excitement. "I could ask the boys to help without telling them about the Huntingtons."

Libby nodded. She tried to act excited, but she couldn't. She was glad when Chuck opened the pickup and climbed inside. He smelled of peppermint candy.

"Here you go, Elizabeth." Chuck smiled as he handed the pack of pictures to Libby.

"Oh, this is exciting!" cried Susan. "Hurry, Libby! I want to see the pictures!"

Chuck drove away from the curb as Libby opened the envelope nervously. She pulled out the stack of snapshots and gazed at a picture of Snowball beside the barn. The green background of grass and trees showed off Snowball's white hair. Her mane was neatly brushed, and her forelock hung neatly between her eyes. The picture was so lifelike Libby couldn't quit looking at it. Finally she looked through the others. Some of them weren't as good, but most of them had turned out well. She laughed aloud at the picture of the striped kittens peeking over the hay. "Look! Oh, aren't they cute!" Libby handed the picture to Susan, and she laughed and showed it to Chuck.

"You're going to have a hard time picking the best one out of that batch," said Chuck.

"Mom will love them all!" cried Susan as she looked through the pictures again.

Libby glowed with pride. She hadn't thought the pictures would turn out so well. She probably wouldn't have to take any more for the contest. Suddenly she realized that if she told anyone that, she'd have no reason not to loan Ben her camera. Her face tightened as she glanced out the window and watched trees, farms, and mailboxes pass. At the Bender's farm a black dog ran out to bark at the tires.

"That dog will get hit one of these days," said Chuck. He said the same thing everytime he drove past and the dog barked at their tires.

"The Benders should tie the dog up," said Susan.

Libby watched the dog finally give up and run back to the farmhouse.

Later at the Johnson farm Libby showed the snapshots to Vera and the boys. Libby sat at the kitchen table and bit into a crisp apple while the

others talked. Libby usually liked sitting in the kitchen to talk with everyone, but today she wanted to be off by herself, where she wouldn't have to think about how terrible she was.

Suddenly Susan turned to Ben and Kevin. "Could Libby and I trade times with you to go to the store? We'd like to go again tomorrow. It's really important."

Libby locked her icy hands in her lap. She couldn't look at Ben.

"What's so important?" asked Ben.

Libby's stomach fluttered as she waited for Susan's answer. The Johnsons never lied, so she couldn't imagine what Susan would say.

"Libby and I have decided to help the homeless by buying groceries for some of them," said Susan, her cheeks red and her eyes sparkling.

Libby bit her lip. *She* had not decided to do any such thing!

Chuck said, "That's very kind of you."

"How wonderful!" Vera hugged Susan and reached over and patted Libby's arm. "I'll help by giving you $20."

"Would you boys like to help?" asked Susan, looking at Ben, Kevin, and Toby.

Ben and Kevin nodded. Toby said, "I don't have any money."

"What did you do with your allowance?" asked Chuck.

"Spent it," said Toby, looking down at the table.

"All of it?" asked Chuck.

"I have a quarter left," said Toby in a small voice. "But that's not enough to give."

Chuck smiled at Toby. "If you want to give it, it's enough to give. Jesus loves a cheerful giver. He sees your heart when you give. The amount isn't important." Chuck leaned back in his chair and locked his hands behind his head. "There's a story in the Bible about a widow who gave two mites."

"Like the mites on a sparrow," said Ben with a chuckle.

Everyone laughed except Libby, and she couldn't manage even a smile. She knew the mites on a sparrow were tiny bugs, but the mites the woman gave were coins.

"There were others who gave gifts of great value," continued Chuck. "Jesus said the widow gave more than the others because she gave all she had. The disciples had a hard time understanding that. But we know it means Jesus knew what an unselfish person the widow was. Jesus wants you to give, Toby, even if it's only a quarter."

Toby smiled. "Then I'll give my quarter."

"I wonder how many mites in a quarter?" asked

Kevin, his eyes twinkling behind his glasses. "Or on a quarter?"

"How many sparrows can fit on a quarter?" asked Ben, laughing. "There are a lot of mites on each sparrow."

Libby watched the others laugh. She tried to finish her apple, but it stuck in her throat. She didn't want to give even a quarter of her own money away for any reason. She wanted to buy more film for her camera and that new halter for Snowball. The halter! Libby sank lower in her chair. Brenda Wilkens had bought her halter! And Brenda didn't even own a horse!

"Will you boys change days with us?" asked Susan.

"Sure," said Kevin.

"It doesn't matter to me," said Ben with a shrug.

Libby glanced in surprise at Ben. He hadn't even said he'd trade if she'd let him use her camera. That's what she would've done.

Just then Rex, the Johnson's black and tan collie, barked outside the back door to let them know someone was coming. Ben ran to the window and looked out. "It's Brenda and Joe."

Libby's jaw tightened as she jumped up and followed the Johnson kids outdoors. Goosy Poosy honked from inside the chicken pen. Libby watched

Brenda run up to Ben with the halter in her hand. Joe stopped beside Susan.

"Look what I got today," said Brenda, holding up the halter.

"I like it," said Ben.

"It came from your dad's store," said Brenda, looking right at Libby.

Libby lifted her chin. Somehow she'd convince Brenda to let her buy the halter from her.

"We could try it on Snowball to see how it'd look," said Brenda.

Libby doubled her fists at her sides.

"We don't even have a horse yet," said Joe. He was thirteen and had dark brown hair and brown eyes. He wore a white tee shirt and tan shorts. He smiled at Libby. "When we do get a horse, I'd like one just like Snowball."

"I want one like Star," said Brenda. Star was Ben's horse, and Brenda always liked anything of Ben's.

"Try the halter on Star, not Snowball," said Libby sharply.

Brenda shook her head. "No. It looks like it was made for Snowball." Brenda laughed wickedly.

Libby's temper shot up, but she didn't punch Brenda.

Susan stepped closer to Libby. "We can go back inside if you want," Susan whispered.

Libby smiled weakly at Susan, but shook her head. She didn't want Brenda to think she could force her out of her own yard.

Slowly Libby followed the others to the pen behind the horse barn. Snowball nickered and ran to the fence. She looked clean and bright. Libby smiled proudly. She'd never even touched a horse until she'd come to live with the Johnsons. Having a horse of her very own still seemed too good to be true.

Joe leaned against the fence beside Libby. "What did Brenda do to you this time?" he asked softly.

Libby shrugged as tears pricked her eyes from Joe's kindness. She couldn't talk around the lump in her throat.

Ben slipped the halter on Snowball, and it looked as perfect as Libby knew it would. "It looks good," said Ben.

Brenda smirked at Libby. Then she turned to Snowball and began to run her fingers over the red and white halter.

Susan stamped her foot. "Brenda, stop being so mean! You didn't even want that halter until I said Libby was going to buy it!"

"So that's it!" cried Joe. "Brenda, you let Libby have that halter or I'm telling Dad."

Brenda flipped her long, dark hair back. "He won't

make me give it to her. It's mine, and I plan to keep it!"

Libby jumped over the fence and frantically tugged at the halter to unbuckle it. Snowball tossed her head, but Libby held on firmly.

"Stop it, Libby!" cried Ben, tugging at Libby's arm.

"Leave me alone!" snapped Libby, jerking away from Ben.

"You're such a baby! Such an aid kid!" said Brenda with a sneer.

Libby slipped the halter off Snowball, then tossed the halter down and ground it into the dust with one foot.

"Don't, Libby!" cried Susan.

Libby watched the bright halter turn dirty and she laughed.

Brenda reached down for the halter, but Libby pushed her away. Brenda fell back and landed right in a pile of manure. "Oh yuk!" She jumped up, her face brick red. "Look what you did!"

Joe laughed and Brenda glared at him. The laugh died in his throat.

Finally Libby picked up the halter and held it out to Ben. "Give this to Brenda."

Ben shook his head. "Libby, you're in trouble now."

"I don't even care!" Libby climbed the fence and jumped down on the other side. But she did care.

She wanted to be like Jesus. He would never stomp on a halter or push Brenda down.

Tears burning her eyes, Libby ran to the house with Brenda yelling after her.

EIGHT
A talk with Chuck

Libby slowly hung up the dish towel. The hum of the dishwasher seemed extra loud. Just after supper Chuck had slipped his arm around her and whispered, "I want to see you in my study when you're finished with the dishes."

Libby sighed. She'd taken as long as she could to dry the dishes that wouldn't fit in the dishwasher. The smell of the roast beef still hung in the air. Piano music drifted out from the family room, where Vera was playing. Ben's loud shout rose from the basement, where he was playing Ping-Pong with Susan. Kevin and Toby were outdoors playing.

Outside Chuck's study Libby took a deep breath, then knocked quietly. She knew Chuck had seen right through her and was going to tell her how terrible she was for being selfish. She didn't want to hear that, nor did she want to part with any of her money.

"Come in," called Chuck.

Libby slipped inside and closed the door after her. Chuck sat behind his big oak desk. Papers were scattered all over it. Chuck had changed into faded jeans and a short-sleeved, pink button-up shirt.

Chuck jumped up and walked around the desk in his stocking feet. He slipped his arm around Libby and led her to the leather couch.

Libby folded her arms across her thin chest and stared down at the carpet. How she wished she was outside with Kevin and Toby!

Chuck laid his arm across the back of the couch and twisted so he could see her as he talked. "Elizabeth, I hear you had a little trouble with Brenda Wilkens a while ago."

Libby stared at him, her mouth open. "Trouble with Brenda?"

"Her father called," said Chuck, cocking one red brow.

Libby flushed, but deep inside she was relieved Chuck wanted to talk about Brenda and not about being selfish. "Brenda was teasing me and being mean again," said Libby.

"I'm sure she was," said Chuck. He took Libby's hand in his. "But even if she is mean and even if she does tease you, you cannot be mean back. You are to love like Jesus loves."

"I know," whispered Libby. She smelled Chuck's after-shave and felt the callus on his palm.

"I want you to apologize to Brenda," Chuck said softly.

Libby gasped. "Do I have to?"

"Yes."

"Even if I'm not really sorry?"

Chuck smiled. "I know you, Elizabeth. I know you're sorry you lost your temper with Brenda. I know you didn't want to be mean to her. Since you've accepted Jesus as your Savior, you've been learning to be like him. I know that, Elizabeth."

Libby blinked back tears. Everything Chuck said was true. "I'll call her," Libby finally whispered.

"Good. I told Mr. Wilkens that." Chuck smiled. "There's more."

Libby's heart sank. Now he'd talk to her about being selfish.

"Mr. Wilkens said the halter is ruined, and he insists he must return it. I said we'd buy it from him since you want it for Snowball."

Libby's mouth fell open.

Chuck laughed. "That surprised you, I see." He sobered. "But, Elizabeth, you must pay for the halter yourself. I'll return Mr. Wilkens's money to him and get the halter. You will pay me for it as you can. You can't have the halter until it's completely paid for. I will let you buy it at my cost. Instead of paying $25.00, you'll pay $19.50."

Libby flung her arms around Chuck and hugged him hard. "I'll pay you every penny! It's a beautiful halter! You should see how great Snowball looks in it!"

"I'm sure she does," said Chuck as he stood up and pulled Libby after him. He looked down at her, and he held her hands. "Elizabeth, you're never alone. Jesus is always with you. When you feel tempted to do wrong, like lose your temper and stomp a halter into the ground, ask Jesus to give you the strength to control yourself. He won't force you to hold your temper, but he'll give you the strength to control it when you ask him. Remember that, will you?"

"I will!" Libby smiled as she wrapped her arms around Chuck's waist and laid her head against his chest. She heard his heart beat against her ear and smelled his special smell. "I love you, Dad," she said confidently.

Chuck hugged her tightly. "I love you, Elizabeth. I'm proud of you!"

Abruptly Libby pulled free and walked from the study, her cheeks burning. He wouldn't be proud if he knew how selfish she was. But now, more than ever, she had to save her money. She wanted the halter for Snowball as soon as possible. She didn't have to wait for the money from the contest. Besides, someone else might win, so she shouldn't even count on that money.

Several minutes later Libby sat at her desk and counted out her money. She had $11.85 instead of $12.00 like she'd thought. She wouldn't buy any more film for her camera. She wouldn't put any offering in for Sunday school or pay tithe at church. And she wouldn't give any money to Susan to help buy groceries for Bobby and Mike. "I'll be able to pay for the halter by the end of the week!"

Just then Susan called, "Libby!"

Libby scooped up her money and dropped it into the top drawer of her desk. She moved the puzzle box from her real dad back in place, then ran to unlock her door.

Susan's cheeks were flushed and her eyes bright. "I beat Ben at Ping-Pong!"

"Great! What happened?" Ben usually won every game he played.

"I guess his mind was on his trip this weekend," said Susan. She sank to the edge of the big, round red hassock and locked her hands around her bare knees.

Libby turned her chair around to face Susan and sat down. "He'll have a lot of fun with Grandpa."

Susan nodded. "I still wish I could go."

"I know." Libby really didn't want to go visit an abandoned copper mine, but she knew she'd have fun with Grandpa. It was always fun to go places with Grandma and Grandpa Johnson.

Susan flipped back her red-gold hair. "Did you decide how much money you'll give for groceries for Bobby and Mike?"

Libby swallowed hard. "Susan, I really feel terrible, but I can't give any."

"What?" cried Susan. "But we planned it all out!"

Libby took a deep breath and told Susan about the halter. "I have to pay for the halter, Susan."

"Dad wouldn't mind waiting another two or three weeks," said Susan.

Libby knew that, but it made her angry that Susan had to bring it up. "I want to pay for the halter as soon as I can! You can get the others to help with the groceries."

"I know, but you wanted to help. What if everyone talked about helping, but never actually did it?"

"Mom said she'd give you money and so did the boys. They won't back out." Libby's stomach knotted. "You'll have enough without my money."

Susan slowly shook her head. "Everybody must help, Libby. Can't you understand that? You could help, too, if you really wanted to."

"I want to pay for the halter."

Susan jumped up. "I wish Brenda would've kept that halter!"

Libby shot out of her chair and scowled at Susan. "You're mean!"

Susan stormed out of the bedroom and slammed the door so hard a picture on Libby's wall bounced out, then settled back in place.

Libby started to reach for Pinky on her bed, then drew her hand back. Susan had given her the big, pink dog when she'd first come to live with the Johnsons.

Just then someone knocked. Libby glared at the door. Was it Susan come back to apologize? Well, she just wouldn't let her in! "Go away, Susan!" cried Libby.

"It's me, Elizabeth," said Ben.

Libby sucked in her breath, then slowly opened the door. "What?" she asked coldly.

Ben pushed his hands deep into his pockets and hunched his thin shoulders. "I still want to use your camera."

"No!"

"It takes such great pictures!"

"I know." Libby moved restlessly.

"I need it for this weekend. Please, Libby!"

Libby shook her head hard and closed the door with a firm snap. "Get your own camera," she said through the door. The words burned deep inside her heart, but she wouldn't take them back.

She walked to her closet and pulled out her camera. She studied it for a long time. Maybe she should let Ben use the camera. She wasn't going to use it now that she couldn't afford film for a while. She held the camera to her. "It's mine," she whispered gruffly. With a flip of her hair she carried the camera to the closet and pushed it back behind a game.

Later, Libby walked slowly downstairs to the family room. Each evening Chuck read the Bible and they all prayed together. Libby wanted to hide in her room. Would Susan and Ben tell on her? She didn't want Chuck to know how selfish she was.

Chuck read part of Luke 6 where it says to love your enemies and do good to those who hate you. He read a verse Libby couldn't remember hearing before about being kind and merciful to the ungrateful and wicked. He also read a verse on giving. Libby tried her best to close her ears. She didn't want to give.

When it was Libby's turn to pray, she could barely say anything. All the words seemed dried up inside her.

At her turn Susan prayed, "Thank you, heavenly Father, that we can give to the homeless. Help us all to do our part."

Libby squirmed. She knew Susan meant her.

"And help the homeless to find jobs and homes," Susan said.

Later in her bedroom, Libby changed into her yellow pajamas and sat at her desk to read her Bible. She always read and prayed by herself before she went to bed. She opened her Bible, and it fell open to Luke 6. The thirty-eighth verse jumped out at her: "For if you give, you will get! Your gift will return to you in full and overflowing measure, pressed down, shaken together to make room for more, and running over. Whatever measure you use to give—large or small—will be used to measure what is given back to you."

Chuck had said the verse didn't mean they were to give to get, but it was a promise from God; when they gave, they'd get.

Libby sighed heavily as she closed her Bible. She wasn't giving at all. Did that mean she wouldn't ever get anything?

"I don't care," whispered Libby fiercely. "I need my money to buy the halter for Snowball!"

Slowly Libby slipped between the sheets. A great sadness rose up inside her, and she turned on her side and curled into a tight ball.

NINE
Lorna Huntington

In the storeroom Libby glanced at Susan. "Are you still mad at me, Susan?"

"I guess not. But I feel so bad that you won't help buy groceries for Bobby and Mike!"

"I'm sorry," whispered Libby as she tugged her blue and white tee shirt down over her blue shorts. "I just can't! But I will help them with their mother. I think we should go talk to Mrs. Huntington as soon as we can."

"Me too." Susan's lip quivered. She fingered the big clip holding her hair on top of her head. "Libby, I didn't mean to be so naughty last night. I'm really sorry."

Libby could only nod. She was the one who was wrong! Couldn't Susan see that? "Let's ask Dad if we can leave now and do our work later. I don't think he'll mind, do you?"

Just then Chuck stuck his head through the storeroom doorway. "What's up, girls? I thought you were going to price some things for me."

"We have an errand to run first," said Susan as she tucked her flowered blouse into her green shorts. "Would that be all right, Dad?"

Chuck shrugged. "I suppose so. Is this about the homeless you're going to feed?"

Libby nodded as Susan said it was.

Chuck reached in his pocket. "Here's my share," he said as he held out a twenty-dollar bill to Susan.

"Thanks, Dad!" Susan beamed as she tucked the money away with the rest she'd collected.

Libby felt worse than the worst person she could think of.

"If I can do anything else to help, let me know," said Chuck, then he closed the door.

Susan grabbed Libby's arm and jumped up and down. "Let's hurry! We're going to help Bobby and Mike today!"

Libby managed a weak smile. She wanted to help the boys, but she felt too selfish to get excited.

Slowly Libby walked out the back door, glad the heat spell had broken and today was pleasant. She walked to the storage shed with Susan and tried the knob, then knocked. "It's Libby and Susan," Libby said. There was no answer.

"I'll check for the key," said Susan. She ran to the loose brick and pulled it out. "It's here!" She trembled as she picked it up, slipped the brick back, then ran to the shed. She unlocked the door and opened it. Heat rushed out along with the smell of a wet bed.

Libby wrinkled her nose as she peeked inside. One sleeping bag was rolled up, and the other was spread over a box to dry out the wet spot. The boys were gone, but Mike's teddy bear lay on the box of clothes, giving a sad, lonely look to the shed. "Let's go talk to Mrs. Huntington," said Libby, backing out of the shed.

"Hello, girls."

Libby spun around as Susan locked the shed door. Mrs. Crabtree stood several feet away, smiling at them. Libby's heart almost dropped to her feet. Had Mrs. Crabtree seen inside the shed? "Hello," said Libby weakly.

"I see you girls found the key to the shed. Did you run across any spiders or mice?" Mrs. Crabtree laughed, almost hiding her eyes behind her round cheeks.

Susan laughed weakly. "I hate spiders!"

"I hate mice!" said Libby. It was the only thing she could think to say.

"Did you girls see anything of Bobby and Mike this morning?" asked Mrs. Crabtree, looking around.

Libby froze. "No. Did you?"

"They came in to say hello, but I told them they had to leave. I felt terrible doing it." Mrs. Crabtree looked ready to cry, then she managed to smile. "I told them I'd come outdoors to talk to them when I had a free minute. This was the first chance I had." She glanced around again. "I wish I could find them. I miss them a lot."

"If we see them, we'll tell them," said Susan.

"We'd better get going," said Libby.

"Not yet," said Susan under her breath.

Libby frowned, but Susan didn't explain the delay. Finally Mrs. Crabtree walked around to the front of the store.

"We can't leave until I put the key back," said Susan. "If the boys come, they can't get in without it." She looked around to make sure no one was nearby. Then she pulled out the loose brick and hid the key again.

Libby breathed a sigh of relief. It would be terrible if someone else found the hidden key.

Several minutes later Libby rang the doorbell at the Huntington house. "I hope she's home."

Susan looked all around. "I see the neighbor sitting out by her swimming pool. We could ask her about Lorna Huntington."

Libby waited a while, then rang the doorbell again. "I like her flowers," Libby said, motioning to all the bright flowers along the side of the house and the beds of flowers throughout the yard.

"She probably has a gardener," said Susan. "It takes a lot of work to keep weeds out of all that. I know." Susan hated weeding the garden more than any other job. And Vera always had a large vegetable garden as well as several flower beds.

"I guess she's not home," said Libby. "Or she's not answering her door."

"Shall we talk to the neighbor lady?"

Libby nodded as she led the way across the lush green lawn to the woman sitting on a white lawn chair at the side of a swimming pool.

The woman slid her sunglasses down her nose and looked closely at the girls. She was about the same age as Lorna Huntington and wore a light blue swimsuit. "What can I do for you girls today?" she asked in a pleasant voice.

"We were looking for Mrs. Huntington," said Libby.

"She drove out about fifteen minutes ago," the woman said.

"Do you know when she'll be back?" asked Susan.

"No, but if you're selling something, I don't think she'll be interested."

"Oh, we're not selling anything," Libby said quickly. "We're friends of Bobby and Mike."

"That's right," Susan said, and the woman looked at them, suddenly interested.

"Do you know where the boys are?" she asked.

"We wanted to talk with Mrs. Huntington," Libby added, looking at Susan sideways, "to ask her if she really was as mean to the boys as they said she was."

Susan and the woman both looked at Libby— Susan in surprise, the woman in annoyance. "That's ridiculous," the woman remarked. "I've never known Lorna to be mean to the boys."

"Well," Libby continued, despite Susan's glare at her, "the boys told us that before their parents' divorce, their mom used to scream at their dad."

"He worked all the time, and she got tired of that," the woman said. "Can't say as I blame her."

"The boys love him a lot," said Susan, rising to defend the boys' dad.

"He spent his Sundays with them," said the woman. "Lorna didn't think it was fair. He had time for them, but not her."

"Didn't he love her?" asked Libby. She remembered all the times Mother had said Dad never loved her.

The woman shrugged. "I thought he did. She was very insecure." The woman frowned. "I don't know if I should be telling you girls all this information."

"We're just trying to help the family," said Susan quickly.

"That may be so, but I don't think I want to say anything more," the woman remarked coldly, slipping on her sunglasses.

Just then a car drove into the Huntington's drive. "She's home," said Libby, nudging Susan.

Susan said, "Thank you for all of your help."

Libby ran across the lawn with Susan and stopped beside the BMW just as Lorna Huntington closed the car door.

"What are you two doing here again?" Lorna asked.

"We want to help you find your boys," said Libby.

Lorna's eyes filled with tears. "I don't know why. I don't even know you."

"We like to help others," said Susan. "Jesus wants us to."

Lorna dabbed her eyes with a tissue from her white leather purse. "My mom always said that, but I guess I forgot it."

"Mrs. Huntington, why did you keep this big house when Mr. Huntington doesn't even have a place to live?" asked Libby.

"That's a strange thing to say," said Lorna, study-ing Libby closely. "He has his apartment."

"He lost his job, and he can't afford an apartment," said Susan.

"But that's terrible! I never knew that." Lorna ner-vously pushed her long hair back.

"How long have the boys been gone?" asked Libby.

"They were gone a lot after school but always came home before dark. Then suddenly they left home last week and didn't come back. I was sure they were with Allen, but when I tried to call him, I just got a message that his phone had been discon-nected. Finally I called the police. I didn't want to get Allen in trouble, but I didn't know what else to do. The police have been looking for the boys and Allen—but it was as though they had disappeared without a trace! I've been so worried. When you said you saw them at the general store, I rushed right over there hoping I would find them. But there was no sign of them anywhere. And now to find that Allen doesn't even have a home . . ." Lorna pressed her fin-gers to her mouth and blinked back tears. "Nothing is going right!"

"Our mom would be glad to come talk to you to help you," said Susan. "Her name is Vera Johnson."

"Vera Johnson," said Lorna thoughtfully. "Oh, I

remember her! I met her in school. Her son Toby and my son Bobby are in the same grade!"

"We'll call her to come help you," said Libby.

"She wouldn't want to bother," said Lorna tiredly.

"She'd love to help you!" cried Susan. "She would!"

"I could go see her," said Lorna slowly.

Libby quickly told Lorna the address and how to get to the Johnson farm. "Mom will be happy to see you."

"If you're sure," said Lorna hesitantly.

"May I use your phone to call her?" asked Libby.

"Of course! Come with me." Lorna led the way inside and motioned to a white phone on the wall near the back door.

Libby quickly pressed the numbers, and Vera answered on the first ring. Libby told her about Lorna Huntington.

"Let me speak with her," said Vera.

Libby held the phone out to Lorna, and she hesitantly took it.

Susan smiled at Libby as if to say the job was well done.

Trembling, Libby locked her fingers together and waited while Lorna and Vera talked.

Finally Lorna hung up and wiped her eyes again with a tissue. "She said to come right out, so I'm going to. Thank you, girls. You've helped me more than you'll ever know."

Susan beamed with pride.

Libby felt good for the first time since yesterday.

"Can I drive you girls somewhere?" asked Lorna.

"We were going to the general store," said Susan.

"I'll give you a lift then," said Lorna.

Several minutes later Lorna stopped outside the general store. Libby and Susan thanked her and slipped from the car. Libby glanced nervously toward the storage shed, but the boys weren't in sight.

After Lorna drove away, Susan whispered, "Let's go check the shed again."

Libby nodded. They ran to the shed and knocked on the door, then waited for an answer.

"I hope nothing happened to the boys," said Susan quietly.

Libby's stomach tightened. She searched for the key and unlocked the shed. It was just as they'd left it earlier. She closed and locked the door and put the key back.

"We'll get our work done, then buy the groceries for them," said Susan.

"Buy groceries," muttered Libby. A great weight settled down on her as she followed Susan into the store.

TEN
Allen Huntington

Libby hung back as Mrs. Crabtree rang up Susan's groceries.

Chuck slipped his arm around Libby's shoulder and she jumped. "Why the long face, Elizabeth?"

She couldn't tell him what was really bothering her, so she said, "It's sad to think of the homeless."

"It sure is! I'm glad we could do a little to help."

Libby bit her lip. "What about the people who can't give money to help?"

Chuck pulled Libby tighter to his side. "There's more ways to give than just money. Some people give their time. Others pray for the homeless."

"I never thought of that," said Libby, seeing a little hope for herself. She had prayed for Bobby and Mike, and she had spent her time trying to help them.

"Giving is a part of being a Christian," said Chuck.

"God taught us to give by giving us his greatest gift— Jesus, his only Son. Then Jesus willingly gave his life for us."

Tears burned Libby's eyes as she watched Susan and Mrs. Crabtree and listened to Chuck. It was always a thrill to think God actually gave Jesus so she could have eternal life.

"It's fun to give, Elizabeth. It's a privilege, too. It's another way to be like Jesus." Chuck kissed the top of Libby's head. "I'm glad you're a giver!"

His words wrapped around Libby's heart, and she smiled. "Some people don't give money. Does that matter?"

Chuck shrugged. "As Christians we know to pay our tithe and to give our offerings. The Lord also says to give to the poor. It is important to give money, too, if you can."

Libby's stomach knotted. She had begun to think she'd given all that was expected of her. But that didn't change anything! She didn't have money to give. She'd pray more and help more, but she wouldn't give any of her money!

"There's a customer who needs my help," said Chuck. "I'll talk to you later, Elizabeth."

"Later," whispered Libby. She ran to help Susan carry the two bags of groceries as she tried to forget what Chuck had said.

"I made sure to buy things that don't need to be kept cold," Susan said as they walked outdoors. "I wanted to buy milk, but how could I? It would turn sour in one day in the heat of the shed."

"I noticed you bought a can opener and some plastic spoons. That was smart."

Susan smiled happily. "Thanks. I knew they'd need a way to open the canned fruit I bought them. We'll have to show the boys how to use the can opener."

At the shed Libby knocked, but there was no answer. "That's strange," she said. "Where could they be?"

Susan unlocked the shed and quickly set the food inside, then locked the door again and hid the key. "If they're not back when we finish our work, we'd better look for them."

"They said they spend a lot of time at the park," said Libby. "Maybe they're at the park now."

"Maybe," said Susan.

"I guess we'd better get to work," said Libby, walking into the storeroom. Mrs. Crabtree walked in from the other door. She looked worried.

"Is something wrong, Mrs. Crabtree?" asked Susan.

"The boys still haven't come back! And they said they would." Mrs. Crabtree smoothed the sleeves of her blue work smock that she wore over her white blouse and gray slacks. "Did you girls see them?"

"No," said Libby.

"We'll look again after we stock the shelves," said Susan.

Mrs. Crabtree sighed and shook her head. "They're so little to be on their own so much! I can't understand their mother letting them roam the streets. Someone could snatch them. Or they could get hit by a car! If they were my boys, you'd better believe I'd know where they were at all times!" Mrs. Crabtree turned on her heels and walked back into the store.

"She's really worried," said Susan.

"Let's hurry so we can go look for them," said Libby, suddenly feeling frightened for the boys, too.

For the next two hours Libby worked as fast as she could as she and Susan priced boxes of goods and stacked them on the shelves. They didn't take time to whisper and giggle as they usually did as they worked. Twice Chuck gave them more work, but they kept at it without complaining until it was finished.

Finally Libby tossed the last empty box in the dumpster. "Now we can check on the boys, Susan," Libby said, her face flushed and a smudge of ink on her cheek.

Susan ran to the loose brick and tugged it free. Her eyes widened. "Oh, Libby, look!"

Libby peered over Susan's shoulder. "The key is

gone," whispered Libby, sighing in great relief. "The boys are back!"

Libby ran to the shed with Susan at her heels. Libby knocked and said, "Bobby, Mike, open the door!"

The door didn't open, and the boys didn't answer.

Susan knocked. "Bobby, Mike, it's all right. It's Susan and Libby. We want to talk to you."

Suddenly the door burst open, but Bobby and Mike didn't stand there. Instead it was a short, thin man with blond hair and blue eyes. He looked frightened. "How do you know about my boys?" he demanded.

Libby gasped and Susan fell back a step. "Are you Mr. Huntington?" asked Libby barely above a whisper.

"Yes. How did you know?" Allen Huntington stabbed his fingers through his blond hair, spiking it. "What do you know about my boys?"

"We'd better get out of sight," said Susan.

"We don't want anyone to know you're living in the shed," said Libby.

Allen sighed heavily. "I don't want it known either. It's too small and crowded to talk inside. Can't we talk somewhere else?"

Susan nodded. "Inside the storeroom."

Libby led the way to the break table in the storeroom. She sat beside Susan and across from Mr. Huntington. Libby quickly told him how they'd found the key and everything that led to sending Lorna to the Johnson farm. Susan added bits of information from time to time.

"So you're the ones who left the groceries," said Allen. "They gave me a bit of a scare. I thought the boys stole them."

"They didn't," said Susan.

"Where are the boys?" asked Allen.

"Don't you know?" asked Libby in alarm as she leaned forward.

"I thought they'd be here," said Allen weakly. "I told them I'd be back by noon."

"I thought you got back after five," said Libby.

"I did until today. My job ended today." Allen sounded defeated. "I don't know if I'll be working tomorrow."

"You need help," said Susan, sounding just like Vera.

"I need a job!" replied Allen.

"You need a home, too," said Libby softly.

Allen sagged in his chair. "I'll have to force the boys to go back with their mother even if she won't let me see them again. They can't keep living on the street with me."

Just then Chuck walked in. He stopped short. "What's going on here?" he asked sharply.

Libby jumped up. "Dad, this is Mr. Huntington."

"Bobby's and Mike's dad," said Susan.

"This is our dad, Chuck Johnson, the owner of this store," said Libby.

Allen slowly stood. "Hello."

Chuck shook hands with Allen. "I can see my girls have decided to help out here. I suppose they told you about your boys shoplifting and your wife paying the bill."

Allen sank to his chair and shook his head helplessly. "I thought your girls gave us the two bags of groceries."

Chuck frowned. "I think we're talking about different groceries here." He looked at Libby, then Susan. "Is this the family you're helping?"

"Yes," said Susan.

"Well, well," said Chuck as he sat down across from Allen. "Suppose you fill me in on everything."

"I was director of marketing at Lantee's Baby Wear until just a few months ago," said Allen. "The company had to cut back, and I was one of the first to go. When I lost my job I couldn't continue to keep an apartment, plus pay child support. That's why I moved into your storage shed."

"You live in my storage shed?" asked Chuck in shock.

Libby glanced at Susan, then quickly away. She couldn't look at Chuck.

"I thought you knew since your girls did," said Allen.

"No. No, I certainly did not know!" Chuck looked right at Libby, then turned to Susan. Finally he looked back at Allen. "It's not a fit place to live."

"I know," said Allen weakly. "And when the boys came to stay with me, it made it even harder."

"The boys live in the shed, too?" cried Chuck.

Libby groaned and Susan flushed.

Allen nodded. "I found the key in the lock of the shed a couple of months ago. So I moved in."

"We found the key hidden behind a loose brick," said Libby.

Chuck blew out his breath. "What else?"

"Bobby found the loose brick, and we decided it was a good place to hide the key so it would be there for us," said Allen.

"Couldn't you settle things with your wife and move back home?" asked Chuck.

Allen shrugged his narrow shoulders. "We're divorced; she won't talk to me."

"She said she's been trying to reach you," said Libby.

"I didn't know that," said Allen in surprise. "I finally quit trying. The boys said she didn't want them any longer. I did try to call her to let her know they were with me."

"She thought you still had your job," said Susan. "She tried to call you there and then at your apartment."

"She was very worried about the boys," said Libby.

Chuck reached over and patted Susan, then Libby. "I want to talk to Mr. Huntington privately. Could you girls leave us alone?"

Libby jumped up. "You won't turn him in for living in the shed, will you, Dad?"

"He won't," said Susan as she walked toward the outside door. She stopped and looked back at Chuck. "You'll help him, won't you, Dad?"

Chuck grinned and nodded.

Allen said, "Girls, thanks for your help."

Libby smiled and ran outside after Susan. "Now they won't have to live in the shed. Maybe Dad will let them stay with us."

"He might. Or maybe he'll help get Allen and Lorna back together." Susan pressed her hands to her heart and closed her eyes. "Wouldn't that be perfect for the boys?"

"I wonder where they are?" asked Libby as she scanned the parking lot, the street, and as far as she could see around the residential area. A shiver of fear ran down her spine. Had something dreadful happened to Bobby and Mike?

ELEVEN
Danger!

Libby stopped at the edge of the park and looked toward the tennis courts, then the picnic tables, and the playground. She turned to Susan with a disappointed look. "I don't see Bobby or Mike."

"I don't either," said Susan, puffing from running most of the way to the park.

"Maybe they're on the hiking trail," said Libby. She knew a lot of people liked to walk the trail through the trees.

"Look! There's Marsha Pratt." Susan lifted her arm in a wave.

Wrinkling her nose, Libby watched Marsha as she ran toward them. She was in the same grade as Libby and Susan and she never stopped talking. Libby hadn't seen her since school was out for the summer, and she wouldn't mind never seeing her again.

Marsha grabbed Susan's hand and screamed in glee. "It's so good to see you! You too, Libby."

"What're you doing for the summer?" asked Susan.

"Next week we're going to Prince Edward Island to see the house where Anne of Green Gables lived! Isn't that the most romantic thing you've ever heard of?" Marsha giggled.

"Oh, I'd love to visit Prince Edward Island!" cried Susan. "I watched the 'Anne' videos five times already!"

Marsha pushed back her long dark hair. "I've watched them *ten* times!"

Libby rolled her eyes. She loved watching the video of "Anne," too, but she certainly hadn't watched it ten times, nor did she think Marsha had. "Marsha, have you seen two boys, nine and ten years old? One has brown hair and one blond. They both have brown eyes, and they're short and thin."

"We need to find them," said Susan.

Marsha thought for a moment. "I saw a bunch of boys down by the creek, but I don't know if the boys you want were with them."

"Thanks, Marsha," said Susan. "We'll go see."

"Have fun in Canada," said Libby.

Marsha looked at Libby strangely. "Canada? We aren't going to Canada."

"Prince Edward Island is in Canada, Marsha," said Susan softly.

Marsha grinned sheepishly. "Oh." She shrugged. "See you girls when school starts." With a wave she ran across the park toward the street.

"Let's go," said Libby. She ran past the picnic area and down the incline to the edge of the muddy creek. The water was low because of the hot weather. A green frog jumped in the water with a splash. Libby heard boys shouting around the bend in the creek.

"Libby, do you think we should go where those boys are?" asked Susan, her face pale. "You know how bad some of the boys are who hang out at the park."

Libby nodded as a shiver ran down her spine. She'd heard stories of drugs being used at the park. "We can't quit looking for Bobby and Mike just because we're a little scared, Susan."

"I know." Susan took a deep, steadying breath. "I'm glad Jesus is with us, and we have angels watching over us."

Libby walked carefully through the weeds at the edge of the creek. She heard Susan behind her and the boys up ahead of her. She smelled the fishy smell of the creek and caught an occasional whiff of pine from the pine trees across the creek. Weeds scratched her bare legs, and she wished she was wearing jeans today instead of shorts.

"Don't walk so fast, Libby," said Susan, puffing along behind.

Libby glanced back, then waited for Susan. Libby's legs were much longer than Susan's, so she naturally walked faster. Susan didn't like the feel of the weeds against her legs, so she picked her way carefully instead of pushing through like Libby did.

With loud cries a gang of boys suddenly ran around the bend right toward Libby and Susan. Libby felt rooted to the spot.

Susan tugged on Libby's arm and hissed, "Move, Libby! Come on!"

Libby and Susan stepped up toward the bank away from the creek as the boys ran past, laughing and swearing. "I didn't see Bobby or Mike, did you, Susan?" asked Libby.

"No," Susan said weakly. "I'm sure glad those boys didn't pay any attention to us."

Libby jumped back down to the edge of the creek and walked along it around the bend. She saw the trampled weeds where the boys had stood, but no one was in sight. "Maybe Bobby and Mike didn't come to the park," said Libby in defeat.

"Maybe not," said Susan with a loud sigh.

Libby wanted to say she was giving up and they

should go back to the store, but instead she said, "Let's keep looking."

"Let's do." Susan picked up a stone and pitched it into the muddy water. Ripples widened out until they touched both sides of the creek.

Just then Libby heard a scream. Fear pricked her skin and she gripped Susan's arm. "Come on!"

They raced in the direction of the scream, down the creek where the boys had gone. Libby caught a glimpse of the gang of boys among some willows. She stopped and motioned for Susan to do the same. "Let's sneak up on them," whispered Libby. "We don't want them to see us."

Susan's cheeks were pink and her eyes sparkled. "Let's hurry and see who screamed and why. I usually never get to be in on anything exciting."

Libby clamped her hand over her mouth to stop a laugh. Sometimes she got mad at Susan, but other times she liked having her as a sister. Right now she was glad they were sisters and they were together on this adventure. "Let's go closer," whispered Libby. "Watch out so you don't step on a twig. The sound of it breaking will give us away."

Libby crept forward, keeping the willows between her and the rowdy boys. When she was close enough to see and hear, she stopped and crouched down.

Susan crouched down beside her and whispered, "What's happening?"

Libby shrugged and held her finger to her lips. She glanced over to the gang and saw two boys drag Bobby toward the creek. Libby's heart almost stopped. Were they going to toss Bobby in?

"Leave Bobby alone!" cried Mike. He was straining to get away from a tall boy who held him back as easily as Mike held his teddy bear.

Susan sucked in her breath. Her lips moved, and Libby knew Susan was praying.

Libby knotted her fists. What could they do to help Bobby and Mike? Silently she prayed for the Lord to show her a way to help the boys. She watched Bobby break free and try to run, but the boys caught him again and dragged him right to the very edge of the water. Suddenly Libby had an idea. She whispered her plan to Susan, and Susan giggled under her breath.

Slowly Libby stood, leaving Susan where she was. Libby trembled as she cupped her hands around her mouth. "Bobby!" she shouted. "Mike! Dad says to come here right now!"

The boys gasped. Bobby and Mike looked surprised. Libby walked into sight. She shook her finger at Bobby, then at Mike. "Why didn't you come? You can't play any longer. Dad wants you right now! He said if you're not back in a couple of minutes, he'll come after you himself."

"Libby!" cried Bobby.

Looking guilty, the boys let go of Bobby and stepped back.

Before Bobby could say another word, Libby grabbed his arm. "You get right to the car! I mean it! Susan is looking all over for you."

"Bobby!" shouted Susan, sounding angry. "Hurry up! Mike! Come on!"

Mike pulled away from the boy holding him and ran to Libby. "I wasn't scared a bit!" he said, running to her.

Her face suddenly pale, Libby slipped her arm around Mike. She'd recognized the boy who had held Mike. It was Brent Pulley from school. If he recognized her, her plan wouldn't work.

Libby shook Mike's arm. "Let's go, Mike. Bobby. You knew you could play only an hour. Time is up! We have to get right to the car before Dad comes. You know what he'll do if he has to come after us." Libby shivered. She darted a look at the other boys who were standing together in a tight, silent huddle.

"Bobby! Mike!" shouted Susan again. "Hurry up!"

"We'd better run fast," said Libby to Bobby and Mike. She pushed them ahead of her, and they ran toward Susan.

Susan grabbed them by the hands and ran up the incline toward the park.

Libby glanced over her shoulder, then stumbled and almost fell when she saw the boys racing after them with Brent in the lead.

"I know you, Libby Dobbs," Brent Pulley shouted. "Those little kids aren't your brothers! We'll get you for this!"

Libby scrambled up the incline and reached the smooth ground of the park. She raced after Susan and the boys. She had told Susan not to stop running until they were away from the park.

Behind her Libby heard shouts and the pounding feet of the boys. She could almost feel them grab her. She didn't dare look back or she'd lose stride and waste valuable time. Suddenly she tripped on a rise in the ground. She stumbled, and before she could catch herself, she sprawled face forward on the ground. Her breath shot from her in a loud whoosh. Her head spun. She struggled to move but couldn't.

Brent dropped down beside her and the other boys circled her. "You thought you'd get away with that trick, didn't you? Well, you didn't. Now we'll toss *you* in the creek."

Libby groaned. She still couldn't force words out. She saw the dirty sneakers a few inches from her and

smelled Brent's fishy-smelling hands. Libby groaned again.

"Maybe she's really hurt," whispered one of the boys.

"She's faking," snapped Brent as he nudged Libby's shoulder. "You're not really hurt, are you?"

"I'll be OK," Libby finally said hoarsely.

"I told you!" cried Brent.

Libby weakly sat up. The side of her face was scratched and green with grass stains. Her bottom lip was cut and bleeding. The front of her tee shirt was streaked green from the grass.

"She is hurt!" snapped another boy. "I'm not doing anything to her. Come on, guys."

The boys talked a while and finally ran off, leaving only Brent.

"How come you helped those little boys?" asked Brent as he sat beside Libby in the grass.

"Why do you want to know?" asked Libby stiffly.

"I couldn't believe you ran right up to all of us to help those little kids," said Brent with a laugh. "It took a lot of guts."

"Susan and I told their dad we'd try to find them. We couldn't let you guys hurt them."

Brent laughed. "You were pretty brave."

"Thanks." Libby smiled at him. Suddenly she

remembered how Brent liked to take pictures. "Are you going to enter the 'Cute Animal Photo Contest'?"

Brent shrugged. "I thought about it."

"I'm going to. You should. You're good with your camera."

Brent looked at her in surprise. "I never knew anyone noticed."

"I did. The deadline to enter is tomorrow. So you still have time."

Brent grinned. "I think I might. Our neighbor has some cute puppies. And I have some baby hamsters." Brent looked closely at Libby. "Are you hurt?"

"A little, but I'll be all right."

"I'll help you up if you want."

"No. I can make it," said Libby.

"I'll be going then." Brent jumped up and ran off across the park.

Libby painfully pushed herself up. "Heavenly Father, thank you for keeping me safe from those boys," she whispered, then she half-walked, half-ran toward the sidewalk.

TWELVE
The meeting

Her head down, Libby walked slowly along the side-walk toward the store. Houses lined both sides of the streets. Kids played in the yards of some of them. A cat lay in the grass watching a bird. Libby sighed. She'd wanted to witness the meeting between Bobby and Mike and their dad. Libby licked the dried blood off her lip and hooked her hair behind her ears. She glanced up, then gasped excitedly. Susan, Bobby, and Mike were waiting for her at the corner in back of the store!

"Libby!" called Susan, waving her arm high.

Libby waved back, then ran to them. "I'm so glad you waited for me!"

"I thought something bad had happened to you," said Susan as she peered closely at Libby. "Did the boys catch you?"

"Did they hurt you?" asked Mike, catching Libby's hand.

"Did they throw you in the creek?" asked Bobby with a worried frown.

Shaking her head, Libby laughed and squeezed Mike's hand. Quickly she told them what had happened. "Now, we'd better get back into the store."

Libby led the way into the storeroom. Mrs. Crabtree sat at the table with a cup of coffee and a sandwich.

"Bobby! Mike!" Mrs. Crabtree cried as she jumped up and hugged the boys. "I was so worried about you!"

"Some boys jumped us at the park," said Bobby.

"They were real mean," said Mike. "They were going to toss us in the creek, but Libby and Susan stopped them."

Susan told the story while Libby washed her face and hands.

Mrs. Crabtree beamed at the girls. "What brave girls!"

"Where's Dad?" asked Susan.

"Talking with Allen Huntington," said Mrs. Crabtree. "Just let me finish this, and I'll go watch the store so all of you can talk."

Libby handed cans of chilled fruit punch to the boys and Susan. They drank while Mrs. Crabtree ate the last of her sandwich and drank her coffee. She rinsed her cup, kissed the boys, and walked into the store.

Bobby jumped up. "Is Dad angry, Libby?"

Libby shook her head. "I think he's glad we know about you living in the shed. He really feels terrible making you live that way."

"We won't go home!" said Mike stubbornly.

The door opened and Allen rushed in with Chuck right behind him. A tingle ran down Libby's spine.

"Boys, I've been so worried!" Allen hugged the boys to him, then sat at the table with Bobby on one side and Mike on the other.

Chuck smiled at Libby and Susan, then sat down beside them.

Libby locked her hands in her lap and looked around the table.

"We're sorry we stole from you, Mr. Johnson," said Bobby sadly.

"We won't do it again," said Mike.

"I guess you won't!" said Allen, his blue eyes flashing.

"You boys are allowed back in my store," said Chuck, smiling. "I know you won't shoplift again. Your mother was kind and generous enough to pay for what you took."

Bobby's eyes widened. "She did? I thought she was too angry at us to do anything nice."

"She loves you both," said Allen. "Don't ever forget that! She's upset with me, but not with you two."

Libby sighed in relief. She was glad Lorna loved her boys.

"We worked out a plan," said Chuck. "We need you boys to agree to it."

"I won't go home," said Mike firmly.

Libby knew just how he felt.

Allen pulled Mike close. "You'll do what you have to do, Mike. We all will. Chuck has invited me to stay a while with them until I can see where I'm going. You boys must go back with your mom."

The boys cried out, but Allen hushed them. Libby moved restlessly.

"Your mom has custody of you, so you must stay with her." Allen tipped up Mike's chin and looked deep into his eyes. "Why don't you want to go back?"

Tears welled up in Mike's eyes. "She made your study into a bedroom for me, and she makes me sleep there! I want to be back with Bobby. And I want your study to be your study."

Allen blinked moisture from his eyes as he pulled Mike close again. "We'll talk to Mom and see if she'll let you share the room with Bobby again." Allen turned to Bobby. "Is that all right with you?"

" Sure. But Mom won't listen. I told her already, but she said Mike's a big boy and should have his own room." Bobby looked around Allen at Mike. "But Mike's not so big. And he's still scared of the dark."

Libby watched Mike duck his head. She knew he didn't want everyone to know he was afraid of the dark. Just then he looked up and Libby winked at him. He winked back.

Allen smiled at the boys. "Your mom will let you room together again once she understands."

"She'll be here soon to pick you up," said Chuck.

"No!" the boys cried in one voice.

Libby's stomach tightened. She heard Susan gasp.

Allen hugged the boys and kissed them on their heads. "We'll work everything out."

Libby swallowed hard to keep from crying. The only way it would work out would be for Allen and Lorna Huntington to get back together again and be a whole family. Why couldn't Allen and Lorna see that?

Later Libby stood beside Susan and watched as Lorna stepped through the door of the storeroom. Libby trembled as she watched Lorna's face light up at the sight of the boys standing with Allen near Chuck. With a glad cry Lorna ran to them and hugged Bobby, then Mike. She left a lipstick mark on their cheeks where she kissed them. Hesitantly, she smiled at Allen.

"Hello, Allen," Lorna said barely above a whisper.

"Lorna," Allen said stiffly. "The boys are ready to go home with you."

"Good! But first we're all invited to the Johnsons for a cookout." Lorna smiled down at the boys. "You'll like the Johnson farm and all the animals. I'll take you home for baths and a change of clothes." She looked at Allen. "I talked with Vera Johnson about everything, and she helped me understand some things I needed help with. I'm ready to talk to you if you still want to. Would you like to come with us now so we can talk?"

Allen nodded. He turned to Chuck and shook hands with him. "Thank you for the help. I'll get our things out of the shed and ride with Lorna and the boys to your place."

"Fine," said Chuck.

Allen turned to Libby and Susan. "Thanks for your help, too. I'll never forget it. I appreciate the groceries." Allen looked down. "It's hard for me to accept them. It's much harder to receive than give."

Libby couldn't understand that at all. It was much easier for her to get than to give. Maybe it was something only adults understood.

110

The boys said good-bye and waved as they walked out the back door. Libby and Susan waved back.

Later at the Johnson farm Libby stood near the grill and watched Ben turn the chicken. It sputtered and spit and sent up an aroma that made her mouth water. They'd already carried out everything for the picnic. The table was covered. She turned to watch Bobby and Mike playing ball with Kevin and Toby. She saw Lorna and Allen walking around the yard, deep in conversation. Libby wanted to hear everything they said, but she knew she didn't dare listen in. Silently she prayed for them to make the right decision.

"Libby," called Susan softly.

Libby walked to Susan beside the picnic table.

Susan motioned to Allen and Lorna. "I think they'll get back together. They aren't fighting or yelling. Just think! We started off helping two little boys and ended up helping a whole family. Doesn't it make you feel good?"

Libby nodded slightly. She'd feel a whole lot better, though, if she could forget just how selfish she really was.

THIRTEEN
The photo contest

Libby played the song again, only missing one note.
She stroked the piano keys and smiled. Someday
she'd be a famous concert pianist! She'd play for thou-
sands of people, and they'd clap and beg for more.
Maybe the Huntingtons would come to the concert
and tell all their friends that they'd known Libby
since she was twelve and just starting out. They
might say, "Libby helped us when we really needed
help."

Just then Susan walked in. "Mom just told me
Lorna is ready to consider taking Allen back."

"That's wonderful!"

"I'm sure glad Mom and Dad aren't divorced!
Wouldn't it be awful?" Susan perched on the arm of
the couch.

Libby nodded. She couldn't imagine Chuck and

Vera divorced. They said God helped them work out their problems. "Are Bobby and Mike coming over today?"

"Yes. We're watching them so Lorna and Allen can have time alone." Susan pressed her hands to her heart. "Isn't that romantic?"

Libby rolled her eyes.

"Allen gave back the groceries. He said he wanted us to give them to another homeless family. So, Mom's going to help me take the groceries to the right people. You can come if you want."

"Thanks." Libby said with a forced smile.

"I better let you finish practicing. I'll let you know when we're going." Susan ran out, her red-gold hair flipping around her slender shoulders.

Libby sighed. Was it too late to use some of her money for more groceries? Maybe she should give a couple of dollars just to keep from feeling guilty. She shook her head. Chuck had talked about that very thing. "Never give out of guilt," he had said. "Give cheerfully because it's the right thing to do."

In the distance Libby heard the phone ring, then Susan called, "Libby, the phone's for you."

Libby froze. Would Mother call her and beg her to come back to her? Libby bit her lip to hold back a whimper. Or maybe it was Social Services saying they'd made a big mistake and she wasn't really supposed to live with the Johnsons.

"Libby!" called Susan again. "Get the phone!"

Trembling, Libby ran to Chuck's study where she knew she could talk in private. Her hand shook as she picked up the receiver. "Hello."

"Libby? It's Brent. Brent Pulley."

Relieved, Libby sank into Chuck's chair. Brent Pulley! Why would he call her? "Hi Brent," she managed to say.

"I did it, Libby," he said.

"Did what?"

"You know. Entered a photo in the contest. I thought you'd like to know."

"No! Oh no!"

"Didn't you want me to enter after all?" Brent asked stiffly.

"It's not that, Brent! Oh, but it's really, really terrible!" Libby's heart thudded painfully against her chest as she gripped the receiver tightly. "Brent, I forgot to take in my photo! And yesterday was the deadline!"

"Are you kidding? That's too bad, Libby. Are you sure it's too late?"

"I know it is!" Yesterday she'd been so caught up with the Huntingtons that she'd totally forgotten about the contest deadline.

114

"I'm sure sorry, Libby."

"Me, too. I hope your picture wins."

"Me, too. It's really cute." Brent laughed self-consciously. "I wouldn't say that to anyone else, but you understand, don't you?"

"Yes."

"I took a picture of my baby hamsters. One is on its back growling and batting its paws. Two others are all hunched up just looking at the one as if they're asking him what his problem is. I put them beside one of my old sneakers to show how tiny they are. It makes you laugh to look at it."

Libby chuckled as she struggled against feeling sad about her entry. "I'd like to see your picture."

"You would? Really? I kept a copy. I could show you if you want."

"Sure. I'd like that."

"Are you coming into town today?" asked Brent.

"No. But you could come here if you want. Do you know how to get here?"

"Yes. I'll ride my bike and be there before noon." Brent laughed. "I think you'll like the picture."

"I think so, too. See you later." Libby slowly hung up, then walked back to the family room. She felt too depressed to play the piano now.

Just then Ben walked in with a vase of flowers. He set them on the coffee table, then turned to Libby.

He wore faded jeans and a yellow tee shirt. "What's wrong?"

"What do you care?"

"You look ready to cry."

"And you're probably glad of it!" snapped Libby as she flopped down on the couch.

"What's wrong with you, Elizabeth? Why're you mad at me?"

"You'll be glad about what happened to me."

"What?" Ben sat on the piano bench and leaned forward.

Libby flung her arms wide. "I forgot to submit my photo to the 'Cute Animal Photo Contest'! And the deadline was yesterday!"

Ben smiled sheepishly. "I took it in for you."

"You what?" cried Libby, jumping up.

"I tried to call you at the store, but you were gone. So I took the photo in myself. I meant to tell you."

Libby scowled. "Why would you do that?"

"Because I knew you wanted to enter."

"I suppose you entered the very worst shot."

"I did not! I took the one in of Snowball sniffing a kitten."

Libby stared at Ben in shock. "But that's the one I wanted to enter!"

"I thought it would be."

116

Libby frowned, then finally said, "Are you doing this just so I'll let you borrow my camera?"

Ben shook his head. "No. I already know you won't let me use the camera."

"I don't understand you at all!" cried Libby, feeling so guilty she could hardly stand it.

"Why are you so upset?" asked Ben with a puzzled look on his face. "I only wanted to help you."

Libby stamped her foot. "Why are you always so good?"

Ben's face turned as red as his hair. "Do you want me to be mean?"

"Yes! No! Oh, I don't know!" Libby ran from the study and outdoors to the pen where Snowball was. Libby put her arms around Snowball's neck and cried against her dusty, white mane.

FOURTEEN
The camera

Libby sat at the picnic table beside Brent and looked at the photograph of his hamsters. The old blue sneaker made a great background for the blond hamsters. She laughed as she turned to Brent. "This is really good, Brent."

He smiled with pride. "Thanks. I think so, too. It's too bad you didn't get yours entered."

Libby swallowed hard. She had washed away all the signs of her earlier tears. "Well, actually, I did. Ben just told me that he took it in because I forgot to."

"That's great! It makes me feel better."

"Why?"

Brent tugged at the neckline of his gold tee shirt. "I was really rotten to you and you were nice to me. It made me feel even worse."

118

Libby knew exactly what he meant.

"You didn't have to be nice to me or tell me about entering the contest. But you did. I know it's because you're a Christian."

Libby nodded slightly. Sometimes she didn't feel like one at all, but she knew she was because she'd accepted Jesus as her Savior.

Brent slipped the photo back into the envelope. "I'm a Christian too, but sometimes when I hang out with those guys at the park, I start acting like they do. I decided, after you talked to me, I wouldn't do that again."

Libby could hardly believe her ears. Something she had done had affected Brent!

"You didn't yell at me and tell me I was no good," said Brent. "And I knew I was no good. You did something nice for me."

Libby blinked back tears. What she'd done hadn't seemed like much at all, yet it had been to Brent. Maybe entering her photo hadn't been a big deal to Ben. He'd done it because he knew she'd forgotten to, not to show her he was good and she wasn't. She smiled, thankful she finally understood. She really was learning to be like Jesus even when she wasn't thinking about it!

"I'd like to see the pictures you took," said Brent.

"I'll get them," said Libby, jumping up. "Wait here. I'll be right back."

Just then Susan walked out the back door. She wore red shorts and a white tee shirt with red hearts on it. She stopped short when she saw Brent.

"Susan, this is Brent Pulley," said Libby. "He came to show me his photo for the contest. Talk to him while I'm gone, will you?"

"Aren't you the one who was chasing us yesterday at the park?" asked Susan.

Brent flushed and nodded.

"But he's sorry," said Libby.

"I am," said Brent.

Susan shrugged, smiled, and sat beside him. "OK. I'm glad you didn't catch us."

Libby ran inside and didn't hear Brent's answer. In her room she grabbed the pack of photos, then she glanced toward the closet. Slowly she walked to the closet and lifted down her camera. She held it against her heart. Could she let Ben borrow it?

"What if he ruins it?" she whispered. Why should she even consider letting him use it? He wasn't expecting her to change her mind. With a whimper she set the camera on her desk beside the puzzle box, then ran back downstairs and outside.

Brent and Susan were talking and laughing as if they'd always been friends. Libby handed Brent the pack of pictures, then sat down across from him. She locked her hands in her lap as Brent and Susan looked at the pictures together.

"They're all good," said Brent. "I bet it was hard to choose the one for the contest."

"It was," said Libby. She still couldn't believe Ben had picked the very one she had planned to send. She hadn't told anyone her final choice. She'd narrowed it down to three but hadn't decided on the one until she'd gone to bed.

Brent stayed a while longer, then rode away, waving good-bye at the end of the long driveway.

"I like him," said Susan. "He told me how nice you were to him."

Libby wrinkled her nose. "It was nothing."

"It meant a lot to him," said Susan.

Just then Allen Huntington walked out the back door. "I was looking for you girls," he said.

They walked back to the picnic table and sat down. Allen sat across from them. A rooster crowed and Snowball whinnied.

"You look excited about something," said Libby, smiling.

"I am." Allen folded his hands on the table and leaned forward. "Lorna has agreed to talk to a marriage counselor to see if we can patch up our broken marriage. She says I can see the boys every day. And she moved Mike back to Bobby's room."

"That's great!" cried Susan.

"And we've decided, since Mrs. Crabtree and the boys love each other so much, that we'll see they spend some time together. Mrs. Crabtree wants the boys to call her Grandma." Allen smiled.

"I'm glad for all of you," said Libby.

"It all happened because you girls cared enough to help my boys," said Allen.

Libby looked down at her hands. She wished she'd done more.

"We're glad we could help," said Susan.

"Your dad told me about a couple of leads for jobs, so I'll check into them," said Allen. He smiled. "A few days ago life was very bleak. Now there's hope."

Libby heard a car driving in. Goosy Poosy honked, and Rex ran around the house barking.

"It's Lorna and the boys," said Allen with a flush of pleasure.

Libby stayed back as Susan and Allen walked toward the BMW. The boys scrambled out of the car, hugged Allen and Susan, then Mike ran to Libby.

"Hi," Mike said.

Libby smiled down at him. He wore blue shorts and shirt and carried his teddy bear. "Hi."

Mike thrust out his teddy bear. "This is for you."

Libby gasped in shock. "But you love your bear!"

"I know. I want to give him to you since you did so much for me."

Libby sank to the bench and held the floppy bear in her hand. Tears glistened in her eyes. "Mike, you're sweet to give this to me, but I just can't take it. You love it so much, and I don't want you to live without it."

"But I don't have anything else important enough to give you," said Mike. "That's my best thing."

Libby pulled Mike close to her. "Thank you, Mike." She couldn't take his most prized possession! But how could she refuse it without hurting him? Suddenly she had an idea. She stroked Mike's soft blond hair. "I will take your wonderful gift. But I'll need a baby-sitter for him. Would you baby-sit for me? Would you keep the bear with you and take care of him for me? Would that be all right with you?"

Mike looked at his teddy bear and finally nodded.

Libby held the bear out, and Mike carefully took it and hugged it to him. "Thanks, Mike," she whispered.

"You're welcome," he said as he kissed his bear.

Libby blinked back tears. Mike had given something to her of greater value to him than anything he owned. Why couldn't she give that easily?

Later in her room Libby picked up her camera. Tears slipped down her cheeks. "Jesus, I know you want me to share and to give. I do want to be like you and give like you. Forgive me for being selfish." She looked at her camera. "Help me to share my camera with Ben."

Slowly Libby walked to Ben's room and knocked on his door.

"Come in," he called.

She opened the door, hesitated, and walked in. He sat at his desk putting together a model airplane. "Here," she said as she held her camera out to him.

His eyes widened. "Your camera!"

"You can use it," she said softly.

Ben shouted with glee, then took the camera and looked at it as if he'd never seen it before. Finally he looked at Libby. "Thanks, Elizabeth! I'll take good care of it."

"I know," she whispered.

"Why'd you change your mind?" he asked.

"I just did."

"Thanks," he said softly.

Libby nodded. Slowly she walked back to her room and sank to the edge of her bed. She picked up Pinky and held him tight.

Suddenly a bubble of joy burst inside Libby and she laughed aloud. Giving was fun! Next time some-one asked her to give even money she'd be ready to

124

do it. She'd give her best just like Jesus did. "And just like Mike did," she whispered.

Laughing softly, Libby walked to her desk to take out money to give to Susan for groceries for the homeless. It would take longer to pay for Snowball's halter, but it really didn't matter. "Snowball won't care," said Libby as she counted out five dollars.

ABOUT THE AUTHOR

Hilda Stahl was born and raised in the Nebraska Sandhills. When she was a young teen she realized she needed a personal relationship with God, so she accepted Christ into her life. She attended a Bible college where she met her husband, Norman. They and their seven children now live in Michigan.

When Hilda was a young mother with three children, she saw an ad in a magazine for a correspondence course in writing. She took the test, passed it, and soon fell in love with being a writer. She would write whenever she had free time, and she eventually began to sell what she wrote.

Hilda now has books with Tyndale House Publishers (the Elizabeth Gail series, The Tina series, The Teddy Jo series, and the Tyler Twins series), Accent Books (the Wren House mystery series), Bethel Publishing (the Amber Ainslie detective series, and *Gently Touch Sheela Jenkins,* a book for adults on child abuse), and Crossway Books (the Super JAM series for boys and *Sadie Rose and the Daring Escape,* for which she won the 1989 Angel Award). Hilda also has had hundreds of short stories published and has written a radio script for the Children's Bible Hour.

Some of Hilda's books have been translated into foreign languages, including Dutch, Chinese, and Hebrew. And when her first Elizabeth Gail book, *The Mystery at the Johnson Farm,* was made into a movie in 1989, it was a real dream come true for Hilda. She wants her books and their message of God's love and power to reach and help people all over the world. Hilda's writing centers on the truth that no matter what we may experience or face in life, Christ is always the answer.

Hilda speaks on writing at schools and organizations, and she is an instructor for the Institute of Children's Literature. She continues to write, teach, and speak—but mostly to write, because that is what she feels God has called her to do.

*If you've enjoyed the **Elizabeth Gail** series,
double your fun with these delightful heroines!*

Anika Scott

#1 The Impossible Lisa Barnes

#2 Tianna the Terrible

Cassie Perkins

#1 No More Broken Promises

#2 A Forever Friend

#3 A Basket of Roses

#4 A Dream to Cherish

#5 The Much-Adored Sandy Shore

#6 Love Burning Bright

You can find Tyndale books at fine bookstores everywhere.
If you are unable to find these titles at your local bookstore,
you may write for order information to:

**Tyndale House Publishers
Tyndale Family Products Dept.
Box 448
Wheaton, IL 60189**